"It's not my *wish* to marry your brother. Or be kissed by you," she lied.

"That will not happen again," he said with a slight, formal inclination of his head. "As delightful as the diversion was."

In order to make true his promise Rafiq knew he would have to take care to keep her literally at arm's length in future. For some reason his brain ceased to function around her.

He was still shocked to the core that for the first time in his life he had permitted carnal need to overrule common sense and logic.

"You want me to marry your brother, so what was that?" Her hand went to her lips—they still felt swollen and oversensitive. "A test run?" she suggested bitterly. "The Royal bedroom test? Did I pass?'

Gabby took an involuntary step back as fury flashed in his eyes and the pewter flecks were swallowed up as they darkened.

"That was a mistake," he gritted through clenched teeth.

Dear Reader,

Harlequin Presents® is all about passion, power and seduction—along with oodles of wealth and abundant glamour. This is the series of the rich and the superrich. Private jets, luxury cars and international settings that range from the wildly exotic to the bright lights of the big city! We want to whisk you away to the far corners of the globe and allow you to escape to and indulge in a unique world of unforgettable men and passionate romances. There is only one Harlequin Presents. And we promise you the world....

As if this weren't enough, there's more! More of what you love every month. Two weeks after the Presents titles hit the shelves, four Presents EXTRA titles go on sale! Presents EXTRA is selected especially for you—your favorite authors and much-loved themes have been handpicked to create exclusive collections for your reading pleasure. Now there are more excuses to indulge! Each month, there's a new collection to treasure—you won't want to miss out.

Harlequin Presents—still the original and the best!

Best wishes,

The Editors

Kim Lawrence

DESERET PRINCE, BLACKMAILED BRIDE

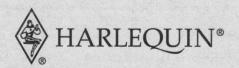

HARLEQUIN®

TORONTO • NEW YORK • LONDON
AMSTERDAM • PARIS • SYDNEY • HAMBURG
STOCKHOLM • ATHENS • TOKYO • MILAN • MADRID
PRAGUE • WARSAW • BUDAPEST • AUCKLAND

Recycling programs
for this product may
not exist in your area.

ISBN-13: 978-0-373-23634-3

DESERT PRINCE, BLACKMAILED BRIDE

First North American Publication 2009.

Copyright © 2009 by Kim Lawrence.

www.eHarlequin.com

Printed in U.S.A.

All about the author…
Kim Lawrence

Though lacking much authentic Welsh blood,
KIM LAWRENCE—from English/Irish stock—
she was born and brought up in north Wales.
She returned there when she married, and her
sons were both born on Anglesey, an island off
the coast. Though not isolated, Anglesey is a little
off the beaten track, but lively Dublin, which
Kim loves, is only a short ferry ride away.

Today they live on the farm her husband was
brought up on. Welsh is the first language of
many people in this area, and Kim's husband
and sons are all bilingual. She is having a lot of
fun, not to mention a few headaches, trying to
learn the language!

With small children, she thought the unsocial
hours of nursing weren't too attractive, so,
encouraged by a husband who thinks she can
do anything she sets her mind to, Kim tried her
hand at writing. Always a keen Harlequin reader,
she felt it was natural for her to write a romance
novel. Now she can't imagine doing anything else.

She is a keen gardener and cook, and enjoys
running—often on the beach because, since she
lives on an island, the sea is never very far away.
She is usually accompanied by her Jack Russell,
Sprout—don't ask, it's a long story!

I'd like to dedicate this book to the memory of my mum, Ann Shirley—lovely lady, best friend, kindest critic and real-life feisty heroine.

CHAPTER ONE

RAFIQ slid his arms into his linen shirt and sat straddling the chair. The pale fabric gaped to reveal the perfectly delineated muscles of his deep gold upper torso—a lot more delineated since he'd dropped almost fifteen pounds.

None of the turbulent seething in his chest was reflected in his expression as, his hands clenched into fists, he fought to control his totally irrational compulsion to drag the grey-haired Frenchman from his seat and throttle a retraction from him.

He was lying—he *had* to be lying!

He didn't, and not just because the doctor was a good twenty years his senior, but because he recognised denial even when he was the one doing the denying. Rafiq knew the man wasn't lying. It was the truth. Not a truth anyone wanted to hear, but the truth.

He wasn't going to see his fiftieth birthday—or, for that matter, his thirty-third!

Once the drumming in his ears had softened to a dull roar a phrase separated itself from the disconnected jumble of thoughts swirling in his head: *roll with the punches*.

It sounded so easy.

Years of practice at rigidly disciplining himself helped, and slowly an icy calm settled over him.

'How long?'

Pierre Henri adjusted his suit jacket—no white coat; he was far too celebrated to need a uniform to establish his authority—and got up slowly. He walked across the room and pulled the X-rays down from the screen, sliding them back into their envelope while he struggled to select his words carefully.

Breaking bad news was a part of the job that he did not enjoy, but it was an integral part of that job and he was considered good at it. He did not normally struggle for words in these circumstances.

He knew the importance of positive body language—it wasn't just what you said but the way you said it—and he knew how emphasising the positive even when there was precious little to be positive about could make a world of difference to the way the person listening felt.

Everyone was different, but years of experience had given him an insight that enabled him to tailor his response to what an individual patient needed from him.

Of course there were exceptions. And this man, he thought, retaking a seat opposite his patient, was one of them!

As his patient's dark eyes locked on to his Pierre felt sweat break out along his upper lip. Insecurity was not something that troubled the eminent physician, yet as he met the pewter-flecked inscrutable gaze of the Crown Prince of Zantara he felt the roles of patient and doctor were oddly reversed.

This man—despite the fact he had just dropped the worst news possible on him—was the one in control.

It was pointless, he knew, to try and understand Rafiq Al Kamil. He was a one-off, a maverick, and neither quality was a feature of his wealth and status—although even for someone like Pierre, who was accustomed to being consulted by the rich and powerful, the sheer scale of the Zantaran royal family's assets was almost surreal.

Pierre was out of his professional comfort zone. Shock, denial, anger—there were as many reactions as there were people. But never in his professional life had he encountered anyone who showed such a total lack of response, and he was thrown.

It was desperately hard to be supportive to someone who appeared not to require any support.

A nicely timed warm handclasp to the shoulder often did wonders, but in this instance he felt any such attempt would be treated as a sign of disrespect—it might even be treasonable!

'I will have to push you, Doctor.'

Pierre started, and coloured at the younger man's prompt.

For the first time the Prince was showing some emotion—and it was impatience. Such control was daunting. This wasn't a display of dispassion, it was… Pierre shook his head slightly as his professional vocabulary failed him. It was *spooky*, he concluded!

He was conscious of feeling more anger and bitterness than this young man was displaying. He had never been able to deliver this sort of news and not feel failure, and this went doubly so when the person concerned should have had his whole life ahead of him, when he was full of life and vigour. It seemed such a tragic waste.

It suddenly occurred to the doctor that the Prince's attitude could stem from the fact that he did not fully comprehend the gravity of his situation. Pierre pushed his glasses further up his nose and angled a kindly look at the tall heir to the throne of Zantara.

'Perhaps I did not explain myself fully, Prince Rafiq?'

'I admit some of the technical language passed over my head.'

I doubt that, thought the Frenchman, not fooled by the self-deprecating response. The intelligence shining in the younger man's eyes was one of the first things he had noticed. And even if he hadn't noticed, it had become clear from the battery of searching questions he had asked that this man had mind like a steel trap.

'Correct me if I am wrong,' Rafiq invited, thinking, *Please correct me. Let this all be a massive misunderstanding.* 'I have a rare blood disorder, and it has reached an advanced stage where there is no hope of cure?' His dark brows lifted towards his hairline. 'There is something else I need to know?' His gesture invited the older man to expand.

Pierre Henri cleared his throat. 'You are probably thinking *Why me?'*

Rafiq's broad shoulders lifted as he stood to tuck the hem of his shirt into the waistband of his trousers. He paused to consider the question before replying. At six-five he towered over the seated man. Broad of shoulder and long of leg, Rafiq's streamlined, muscle-packed frame was athletically formed, and it would have made him stand out even had he *not* possessed a face of startling, symmetrical male beauty, of the type normally seen on classical statues.

'Why not me?' Why should he be exempt from the capricious cruelty of fate? Innocents were given far worse to bear, and he was no innocent—but he *was* a man with a job to do.

He supposed that everyone in his position felt they needed longer—but he really *did* need longer.

'Just so. A very…erm…*healthy* attitude—marvellous philosophy.'

'So, how long do I have?'

Information was power—so they said. Even information you'd have been happier to remain in ignorance of. In Rafiq's mind he equated power with control, and that was a commodity in short supply. He could feel it slipping through his fingers like grains of sand. He could definitely use a little top-up.

The older man's eyes fell. 'Well…erm…these things are very hard to gauge with any precision.'

In other words the news was not good. Rafiq mentally squared his shoulders. 'Make an educated guess.'

'You can, if you wish, have a second opinion.'

Many patients confronted by a diagnosis they did not wish to believe did so—especially those who had the finances to fly doctors from Paris by private jet for a consultation.

'Are you not the best in your field?'

Rafiq was conscious that he ought to be feeling… feeling *what*? More, he supposed. But after the initial kick in the gut moment when he had realised the truth, he had felt very little except a sense of urgency.

'How long do I have?'

'It is hard to be definitive, but I'd say six…'

Rafiq recognised the man's discomfort but felt little sympathy for it. Instead he was conscious of a growing sense of impatience. 'Days? Weeks…? Months…?' None would be long enough to prepare his little brother to step into his shoes.

'Months.'

Nothing in the younger man's demeanour suggested that he had just been given a death sentence.

'Of course the progression of the disease can vary, and if you accepted the palliative treatment we spoke of…'

'This treatment could affect my faculties, my memory?'

The doctor conceded the possibility with a nod. 'It could extend six months to possibly a year, though.'

Rafiq dismissed the suggestion with a wave of his hand. 'Out of the question.'

'I can review your case weekly.'

'As you wish, Doctor.'

'I am so very sorry, Your Highness.'

The offer of sympathy drew a look of cold disdain from the younger man, who sketched a smile and murmured 'You're kind' before excusing himself.

Out in the corridor Rafiq Al Kamil allowed his mask to slip, and his emotions bubbled to the surface in one vicious, corrosive explosion. With a curse he slammed his clenched fist into an innocent wall.

Through his closed eyelids he could still see the pity in the Frenchman's face. Pity. It was one thing that he could not, *would* not endure. He recoiled from the idea of seeing that same expression on the faces of people when they met him.

His jaw hardened and a look of steely determination and pride settled on his patrician features. That wasn't going to happen. Eyes closed, Rafiq expelled the pent-up emotion in one long, sibilant breath. He refused to give way to terror or pity. He would die as he would live—on his own terms. But first there was much to do.

His face set in lines of ruthless resolve, he made his way out into the sunlight. Half an hour later he found himself in the stables, with no recollection of how he came to be there.

Hassan, the groom who had put him on his first horse as a boy, approached.

'Prince Rafiq.' The older man's manner was deferential but not obsequious as he bowed his head.

'Hassan.' Rafiq's smile left his dark eyes bleak. 'You wish me to saddle a horse?'

Rafiq reached out and touched the flank of the mare in the nearest stall. He nodded and said carelessly, 'Why not?'

Riding in the desert was to him the most life-affirming experience possible—and for the moment at least he was still alive. The desert was where he always found himself at times of stress. The sight and sounds of the ageless landscape always cleared his head and restored his focus.

'He is not in the best of moods,' Hassan warned. 'Restless and in need of exercise.' He was looking at the Prince as he said this.

The information was unnecessary as the black stallion being led towards him rolled his eyes, reared up on his hind legs and pawed the air.

'I think perhaps you both are...?' The older man's eyes held a concern he knew better than to express as they scanned the Prince's face.

He had watched the Prince grow from a lively, animated child into the man he was today—strong, resolute, decisive and strong-minded. Yet he was capable of compassion—for all but himself. A man, in short, who embodied all the qualities people expected of a leader, though occasionally in an unguarded moment Hassan fancied he glimpsed briefly the mischievous little boy who had once haunted the stables. The little boy whose passing he regretted.

A man, Hassan reflected, should have a place he could let down his guard, and it saddened him that for his Prince the stables were the closest thing he had to such a sanctuary.

Rafiq stepped forward with a grin. 'I think you are right.' He flashed the groom a warm smile. 'Thank you, Hassan. I will go and change.'

'It is always a pleasure to be of service, Prince Rafiq.'

Gabby identified herself politely. Little option, really, when her path was blocked by two big, bearded men wearing black flowing robes. It had always been her policy to be polite to very large men dressed in black—especially when they were both gripping the jewelled handles of scimitars. Common sense told her the barbaric-looking weapons were purely ornamental—*she hoped*.

Actually, this entire venture was a lesson in hope, but she always had been a 'glass half full' sort of person—though the last two days had cut deeply into her natural optimism.

It was impossible to tell from the larger of the two men's stony expression if he understood a word she was saying, so Gabby repeated herself— this time speaking more slowly and waving her hands descriptively.

'I have an appointment,' she lied. 'I got lost. The King is expecting me.'

The man looked at her in silence, his glance sliding briefly over her dishevelled figure. Gabby was sure guilt and desperation must be written all over her face—she had never really mastered the art of hiding her feelings.

It occurred to her that she should have dressed for the occasion, then her story might not have been met with such obvious scepticism. It was likely people did not take tea with the King of Zantara wearing grubby jeans and a torn shirt.

'I had a slight accident on the way here,' she told the silent man as she lifted a hand to smooth hair that at the best of times refused to be tamed, but just now probably gave her the appearance of an extra in a film that involved mad women and lunatic asylums.

When the man did break his silence it was not to speak to Gabby, whom he regarded with deep suspicion, but to the similarly clad man with him. They conversed briefly in Arabic, then the second man, after sliding a stern look in Gabby's direction, gave a deferential nod of his head to the first and vanished through a door she had not noticed to the left.

Gabby smiled. It was rare that Gabby's smile did not evoke a response from its recipient, but the man in the black robe seemed unfortunately immune to the infectious warmth and her dimple.

'Children and animals like me.'

The limp quip did not draw any response.

He had, she decided, very poor people skills. Maybe being miserable came with the job of protecting the Zantaran royal family from contact with ordinary people? Did they ever step down from their ivory towers?

On the other hand, she conceded, it was possible he knew who she was, and this was the way he treated relatives of almost convicted felons—not that the *almost*, according to the man at the embassy, was anything more than a formality.

As far as he was concerned Paul was as guilty as hell—and this was the man who was meant to be on her brother's side!

'Your brother was caught carrying the drugs, Miss Barton,' he had reminded Gabby, in response to her angry diatribe on the justice system in this dustbowl of a country. 'And Zantara is *not* actually a dustbowl. There are desert areas, obviously, but due to the mountain range to the east and—' He had caught Gabby's eye and cut short the geography lesson, concluding apologetically, 'And in fairness the zero tolerance attitude to drugs here is well known to visitors. Our own government guidelines to travellers actually—'

Gabby, who was not interested in fairness, had cut in, explaining she was not there to read government guidelines but to get her brother out of jail and back home, where she had every intention of throttling him personally.

'My brother is not a drug runner. Stupid, yes,' she conceded. '*Very* stupid,' she added grimly. Only a total imbecile would carry a stuffed toy through Customs for a girl just because she'd smiled at him and looked helpless.

Gabby could see how people found his defence story lame, but they didn't *know* Paul. He had spent his entire adult life being made a fool of by pretty girls, and still he retained his child-like faith in the basic goodness of human nature—especially the human nature of pretty girls. It was left to his sister to be cynical for him.

Predictably, the pretty girl in question this time

had vanished without trace, and now her brother was incarcerated behind prison walls, where he was likely to stay for a very long time unless Gabby pulled off some sort of miracle. And that was looking about as likely as this guard smiling back at her.

She felt the stirrings of despair, and took a deep and sustaining breath before adding another hundred volts to her smile. Stay positive, Gabby, she chided herself. She had to, for Paul's sake, and so far being positive had got her further than any of the embassy man's depressing predictions.

When she had explained her embryonic plan the man at the embassy had laughed. He'd actually given her a patronising pat on the head while explaining that she had to be realistic. It was totally impossible, he'd explained patiently, for her to gain access to the royal palace. As for an audience with the King—well, he had been here twelve months, and that honour had not as yet been granted *him*.

Gabby had asked him if he had any better ideas.

Once he'd starting talking about tact and diplomacy she had tuned him out, deciding there and then she would get into the royal palace if it killed her.

It hadn't—though she did have a few bruises to show for her efforts. She was inside—just— and the place looked as though it was straight from the pages of a fairy tale, complete with minarets that glistened with gold and lapis lazuli in the relentlessly fierce sun that shone down from the dizzyingly blue sky. Another time Gabby might have been enchanted by her surroundings, but she had no time for enchantment. She was on a mission.

First impossible step achieved. The next was to see the man himself—because, as her dad always said, if you wanted something you didn't mess around with the little people, you went right to the top.

And the King seemed about as top as you could get in this oil-rich desert state, and Gabby had every intention of pleading her brother's case to the man himself.

It had been simply bad luck, walking straight into two guards, but hopefully it was only a minor setback.

In deference to her aching face muscles she stopped smiling. She was wondering if it might actually be more useful to play dumb—though it went against the grain—when another granite-faced black-clad figure appeared—thankfully minus a scimitar.

The man with the face like granite looked Gabby up and down. You could almost hear him mentally filing her as harmless before he announced in perfect English that he was going to escort her from the premises.

'I have an appointment with the King.' The more

often she said it, Gabby reflected, the less convincing and more crazy it sounded.

'So I have been told. But there appears to have been a blunder, which I will look into immediately. The King does not have an appointment scheduled today. I am sorry for the inconvenience, Miss…?'

'Barton.'

'Miss Barton. I will have to ask you to leave and reschedule.'

He was scrupulously polite, but clearly—despite the lovely manners—not a man to be messed with. A winning smile was not going to work here.

'Good idea. I'll do that.'

'A wise decision.'

Gabby, who was not renowned for her ability to take no for an answer went meekly, keeping up a steady stream of inanity which after the first few minutes he did not bother responding to, and waited for her chance. Hoping she'd know what to do with it if and when it arrived.

She did.

They had entered a square mosaic-floored hallway—one of several they had passed through—when her escort stopped in response to a call from a short man who was one of the few Gabby had seen not armed to the teeth. As he left her side to speak to the man framed in the arched doorway, it clearly did not cross his mind that his instruction to Gabby to 'Wait there, please' would be ignored.

Gabby flashed her best meek, dumb smile, and waited until he'd reached the other man—then she hit the ground running, and carried on doing just that, ignoring the cries and sounds that followed her as she took the first turning off the wide corridor. Within seconds she was in a maze of narrow corridors, the echo of her heels loud in the silent hallways.

She ran along corridors and up stairs until her knees were jelly, then flopped forward, her long honey-blonde hair brushing the floor as, hands clasped to her thighs, she struggled to drag oxygen into her lungs.

Trying very hard not to think about the abundance of armed men she had seen, she slipped off her shoes, shoving them in the back pocket of her jeans, and continued more cautiously. The corridors were a regular maze, and there were miles of them. Only twice in half an hour did she hear the sound of raised voices and footsteps—presumably a search party after her blood, thought Gabby, though she sincerely hoped not literally.

The third time she heard voices and footsteps they were much closer. Heart pounding, she flattened herself against the wall—as though that was going to make her invisible, she thought, as the pause gave her time to consider her actions.

Her father, who always gave her the benefit of the doubt, would have said she was impetuous. More like reckless and irresponsible, her mother would have retorted, and on this occasion Gabby could see she might have had a point.

What had she achieved?

Beyond the very real possibility there would be two Bartons behind bars by this evening?

Gabby was mad with herself. She knew she ought to have done more research, but when opportunity in the shape of a distracted driver and an open delivery van had presented itself she had reacted without thinking. If she had had more time to plan she might now have an idea of the palace layout.

The sound of a footfall close by interrupted her gloomy analysis of the situation and sent her instinctively for the worn flight of spiral stone steps to her right. She flew up them in breathless haste.

At the top Gabby found herself in a small foyer, with a large metal-studded, ancient-looking door in front of her. At the sound of steps behind her Gabby took a deep breath and pushed it. Relieved when it swung inwards, she stepped inside and, hastily closing it behind her, turned the big key in the lock, shooting home a couple of heavy-duty bolts before leaning back against the solid wood, her chest heaving.

For the first time she looked around the room she stood in. It was curiously shaped—octagonal—but, more importantly from her point of view, it was empty.

As her racing heart slowed Gabby's eyes adjusted to the gloom and she surveyed her sanctuary. Unlike the other rooms she had glimpsed inside the palace it was informally furnished, with an eclectic mix of antique and modern items. One wall appeared to be lined with books, several of which lay open on a large inlaid table, and another wall had heavy curtains pulled across. The light that filtered though the gaps suggested there was a window behind it.

The adrenaline rush that had got her this far abruptly receded, and her knees folded. Spine pressed to the door, she slid down to the floor until she sat, her knees drawn up to her chin, shaking.

CHAPTER TWO

STANDING on the balcony, Rafiq gazed out over the palace's luminous gilded towers and beyond to the city, with its graceful avenues lined by waving palms, its white geometric buildings spreading out into the neatly cultivated fields that had once been desert, and further on again to the purple haze that was the mountain range that ran across the eastern border of Zantara.

It was a view he had looked at countless times, but never before had his appreciation of the beauty held this bitter poignancy.

Zantara had grown beyond recognition in the last few years, but there was still so much to be done—and he had assumed he would be there to do it, to guide his country into the twenty-first century, treading the delicate path between tradition and progress… Frustration and a sense of loss so profound he had no words to describe it clenched around his heart like an iron fist. He closed his eyes, his strong-boned features reflecting the emotions he had fought to subdue since receiving the prognosis earlier.

He jaw hardened, and he dragged a hand through his dark hair while squaring his broad shoulders. He could not afford to indulge in emotional reaction. He needed to stay focused. There was much to do and very little time to do it in.

His task and his title would fall on the shoulders of his younger brother, and his affection for his likeable sibling did not blind him to the fact that Hakim was utterly unsuited to the task.

Zantara was a land richly endowed with natural resources. As well as oil, there were vast mineral deposits as yet untouched. Properly managed, they guaranteed the long-term prosperity of Zantara and its people—but there were many in high places who only paid lip service to the long-term aims that he and his father had always worked towards.

They smiled and applauded reform, but given the chance they would not let morality or ideals get in the way of exploiting the country for their personal gain.

As the heir, over the years Rafiq had been the target of influential families on the make, who would have liked nothing better than to see him marry one of their own, thus automatically gaining—or so they imagined—unprecedented access to the throne.

Zantara had a political stability that was the envy

of surrounding countries, but Rafiq was only too aware of how easily things could change—how little it would take to unbalance that delicate harmony. Introducing a perceived advantage to one of the country's powerful families might be all it took.

Rafiq, who had no intention of allowing that situation to occur, was amused rather than threatened by political manoeuvring. But Hakim was so eager to please, so malleable—in fact all the things that made his brother so much more likeable a person than he was—and he would be putty in the hands of those circling sharks. When Hakim became heir he would become their new target... It was a disaster waiting to happen.

What Hakim needed, he mused, was someone to guide him—someone with backbone, someone behind the throne giving his brother the strength to make tough decisions and see through the sycophants and con-men.

It came to Rafiq in a blinding flash. It was simple, but obvious. His brother needed a wife— the right sort of wife, obviously—who could be groomed for the role of power behind the throne.

Rafiq straightened up as he mentally skimmed the list of possible candidates...

A frown of dissatisfaction furrowed his brow as he methodically discarded them all. It would take a very special woman.

He rubbed a hand over the brown skin of his

neck, feeling the grit that remained after his solitary ride through the desert earlier.

It had required all his considerable skill to stay in the saddle as his Arab stallion, the pride of the stables, possibly picking up on the mood of his master, had spent all the time he wasn't thundering across the desert as though pursued by devils trying to unseat his rider.

The only possible candidate who even began to fill his requirements was—

Rafiq did not complete the thought, because at that moment he heard a voice—a very distinct and very feminine voice.

'So what happens next, Gabby?'

Rafiq knew what was going to happen next, but he could identify with the desperation in that voice.

Either auditory hallucinations were a symptom of the disease the doctor had forgotten to mention, or someone had had the audacity to invade what was his private sanctum. The tower room was the place he retreated to when the weight of the formality involved in fulfilling his duties became too stifling and oppressive—it was his retreat, tucked away in this remote corner of the palace, simply furnished and totally out of bounds.

Utterly astounded that anyone would have such impudence, and curious to see the owner of the very English voice, Rafiq pulled aside the heavy curtain that screened the small balcony from the room beyond.

Chin resting on her knees, Gabby's eyes lifted as the big heavy curtain was swept back, flooding the room with golden light and revealing a balcony surrounded by an elaborately carved railing.

Gabby's eyes carried on up. The golden-skinned man who stood framed in the light-filled arch was seriously tall.

He was also quite spectacularly good to look at.

He wore a knee-length robe in a thin white fabric—thin enough, as a gust of wind plastered it close to his lean torso, for her to make out the shadow of a dark drift of body hair across his broad chest. The riding breeches he wore beneath the robe were tucked into dusty boots. His head was bare and the dusky gloss of his hair outlined by a nimbus of sunlight—which seemed appropriate, as there was something of the fallen angel about his achingly perfect features. Gabby was disastrously side-tracked from her personal dilemma by the combined impact of chiselled cheekbones, a clean-shaven square jaw, a broad, intelligent forehead, aquiline nose, a wide and disturbingly sensual mouth, and in-credible wide-spaced black eyes shot with flecks of platinum and framed by long curling sooty lashes.

Wow!

No man had a right to be *that* good-looking.

He arched a dark brow and drawled. 'Gabby…?'

His voice was deep, and the velvet tones only slightly accented, but for some reason it made the hairs on the nape of Gabby's neck stand on end. Probably the male arrogance he was oozing had got under her skin. Something had. She rubbed her hands along her forearms, troubled by the prickling sensation under her skin.

'No… Yes…' Aware that she was blushing like a schoolgirl, she closed her mouth. Unable to break the mesmeric hold of his bold pewter-flecked stare, she gave up trying to sound like someone with an IQ in single figures.

'You are perhaps bad with names?'

It was not unusual to see a woman in Zantara wearing Western clothes, even though less commonly they wore jeans. But it was very unusual to find one who was blue-eyed or blonde. The young woman sitting on the floor was both.

The startled azure eyes fixed on his face suggested their owner was just as surprised to see him as he was to see her—so this *wasn't* an engineered meeting…

That had been his initial assumption, and Rafiq still reserved judgement. He had been frequently pursued over the years, and the women who set their sights on him constantly managed to surprise him with their ingenuity—not to mention their acting ability.

His vanity, or lack of it, was such that he didn't imagine for one second that it was his personal magnetism that made these women humiliate themselves by going to such embarrassingly elaborate lengths to gain his attention. It was his title, his position that attracted them. The old adage that power was a strong aphrodisiac was not far from the mark.

He had occasionally wondered in the past if he would ever find a woman who wanted him and not what he represented, or even wanted him *despite* what he represented.

Those thoughts had never gone beyond casual speculation, because he had always known that in reality his choice of bride would be a political decision, not a romantic one. His own parents' marriage had been such a one, and despite a considerable age-gap the marriage had been a success. They both respected one another, and neither had entered into the arrangement with any false expectations.

The union had produced two sons, and had done much to negate the political fallout from his father's first marriage. That marriage *had* been a love-match—not in itself a problem, but King Zafir's first wife's inability to supply him with an heir had been. When the King had steadfastly refused to put aside the love of his life, the monarchy that had lasted so many generations had been in real danger. Then, against all the odds, the Queen had conceived, but the country's and the

King's delight had been short-lived. Queen Sadira had gone into premature labour and died of complications. The baby—a boy—had died a week later.

By all accounts his father had been almost mad with grief, and without his powerful hand at the reins the country had divided into warring factions. It had been a time of deep political unrest.

Rafiq had never been able to imagine the man he knew today being so blindly besotted that he'd put romantic love ahead of duty. Even less could he imagine himself repeating that mistake.

Now, of course, the subject was irrelevant. For him there would be no marriage, no wife and no future.

Cutting short this line of thought before he became lost in a morass of despondency, Rafiq dragged a hand though his hair, smoothing the dark strands into the nape of his neck. A frown of distaste drew his brows into a straight line. He despised self-pity in himself even more than in others.

Besides being a pointless emotion, it smacked of self-indulgence—more productive by far to focus on things he could control. Like the blonde…

The blonde whose astonishing neon blue eyes had not yet left his face.

She really was not the sort of woman you would miss in a crowd—not with those eyes and that head of decadent blonde curls that spilled down her back, framing a vivid little face that reminded him of a Titian portrait. But below the neck, he decided, staying with the art analogy, she was pure Degas. Her slim, supple and gently rounded body might have belonged to one of that artist's ethereal ballet dancers.

She looked like a wilted rose, with her grubby face and the purple smudge of exhaustion beneath her eyes. She was the delicate, petite type of female that aroused the protective instinct in a lot of men.

Rafiq's assessing glance drifted from her stubborn chin and defiant, wary eyes to the pouting lower lip, and he thought they would be the same men who failed to notice that she had *stroppy* written all over her.

She began to struggle to her feet. Rafiq noted the tremor in the hand that reached to clutch for support and extended his own. She looked at it for a moment with the sort of enthusiasm that most people reserved for a striking snake, then deliberately ignored it, carrying on struggling.

Rafiq withdrew his hand and with a derisive shrug made no further attempt to help her, even though she looked about as weak and shaky as a newborn kitten.

He liked independent women—but not when they felt the need to make pointless displays of self-sufficiency.

Gretchen, his lover for twelve months previous

to their non-acrimonious split in May, was a highly independent-minded woman, who made no apologies for being ambitious, but she took the little courtesies offered by a man as her due.

Gretchen was a divorce lawyer based in Paris; before her there had been Cynthia, a fashion designer in Milan—long-distance relationships, with women who'd wanted what he did: sex. Not casual, anonymous sex, but sex that came with no emotional strings attached.

Rafiq had never understood why people felt long-distance love affairs put a strain on relationships. For him, the arrangement was perfect. It made it easier to compartmentalise his personal and public life. He never had unrealistic calls on his time when he had duties to perform, there were no draining emotional melodramas, and there were no outside distractions—just mutually satisfying sex.

He was not even sure why he and Gretchen had split up. She was everything he wanted in a woman—totally self-absorbed, of course, but that had its advantages, and she didn't make small talk.

Gretchen hadn't changed, so why had boredom and dissatisfaction set in?

There was never more than one woman in his life at a time, but there generally was one. Sex was important—or it had been! He had put this barren period in his love life down to a jaded appetite. Had his life acquired a certain cyclical predictability?

Was the effort worth the reward? But now, for the first time, he was confronted by the possibility that his recent loss of libido might be another insidious symptom of the disease that was robbing him of his future, of the opportunity to decide that he *wanted* the emotionally draining drama he had been actively avoiding.

He looked at the blonde's mouth and felt his body stir lustfully—and thought maybe not…

He had never been attracted to women who treated their femininity like an affliction, and he got the distinct impression this woman would take it as an insult if a man opened a door for her. She looked all prickles, aggression, and pink sulky lips, he decided, his critical gaze lingering longer than was polite on those lips.

In short, not his type—physically or otherwise. But by anyone's standards she'd definitely fulfil the role of distraction.

It would be a simple matter to have her removed, and that was clearly the logical course of action, but curiosity won out over practicality. How did a blue-eyed blonde come to be in here?

He recognised it was a very poor piece of prioritising, but at that moment this was the mystery that had captured his total attention—maybe he was attracted by its light relief value?

He searched his brain for a plausible explanation for her presence and came up empty. There simply wasn't one. True, tourism was a developing industry in Zantara, but to his knowledge they had not begun offering escorted tours of the palace.

His father was in many ways a moderniser, but the mental image of curious camera-clicking crowds being shown around the King of Zantara's private apartments caused the corner of Rafiq's stern mouth to twitch.

Gabby was conscious of his intense scrutiny—she now understood why people spoke of *feeling* someone's eyes.

Reluctant to reveal her weakened condition to this stranger, she surreptitiously leaned her elbow against an armoire set against the wall. Being a fugitive was certainly exhausting!

It wasn't just her reluctance to show vulnerability that had made her reject his offer of assistance. She couldn't explain it, but the idea of those long brown fingers touching her… She frowned and shook her head, confused by the violence of her gut rejection.

The sound of his bitter-chocolate voice made her jump.

'You are well?'

She tilted her head. He didn't look as if he'd lose much sleep if she said *No, I'm damned well not.* This was not a man who oozed empathy. Under the cool exterior she sensed an explosive, combustible quality that was reflected in his dark stare.

Some women might find that quality attractive, but

she had never felt drawn to dangerous or brooding moody men. He probably practised that expression in front of the mirror, she decided uncharitably.

Gabby dragged a tangled skein of blonde hair back from her face and threw it over her shoulder, pushing back stray tendrils of hair from her sweat-dampened face.

'I'm fine,' she lied, trying to straighten her creased and torn shirt as she continued to regard him warily.

It was a struggle not to show that she was slightly intimidated—all right, a lot more than slightly—by his raw physical presence. Of their own volition her eyes travelled to his toes and made the journey up to his face. A little shudder traced a shivery path up her spine—God, the man had an aura that was almost electric. She had never encountered anything like it—or like him!

'You startled me. I didn't know anyone was in here.'

Not that he was *anyone*. This man was definitely *someone*. She breathed in the outdoorsy scent that drifted from his direction and felt her stomach flip.

His arrogant self-assurance was that of a man who had never heard the word *no* from a woman in his life. This was an alpha male, with raw sex appeal oozing from every pore. He was a man women were programmed to want to say yes to—a man they'd want to father their children. And my goodness, she thought with an inner sigh, as her eyes travelled back to his face, with his gene pool they would be extremely beautiful children.

And so far the utterly gorgeous creature had not opened the door and invited her to leave.

Maybe he wasn't meant to be there either…? she speculated hopefully.

This was an idea she could warm to—and after the last forty-eight hours she needed a break.

She let her fertile imagination go into overdrive. Could this be an upstairs-downstairs situation? Maybe he didn't want to be found out any more than she did? His were definitely the first dusty boots gracing the marble floors she had seen, so it was a real possibility. Had she intruded on a secret assignation?

Admittedly he didn't look like star-crossed lover material—it was sensuality and not sentiment that you saw when you looked at his mouth. Its wide, firm contours sent out a conflicting message of control and passion.

Before Gabby could drag her distracted gaze from his lips and summon up an inventive explanation for her own presence there was a loud bang on the door behind her. Gabby turned and, staring fearfully at the door, began to back away.

'Miss Barton, if you don't open this door immediately I will be forced to break it down.'

No need for that explanation, then.

She wondered uneasily how the tall stranger would react now her fugitive status had been established. She turned her head and was none the wiser. He had a great poker face—actually, he had a great face... Her eyes dropped... A great body...

A great everything!

Despite the uncustomary harassed note, Rafiq immediately identified the voice as belonging to Rashid, a senior member of his father's personal bodyguard—not an easy man to rattle.

He turned his head in time to see a flash of despair and fear in the blonde's wide blue eyes. It only lasted seconds, before she literally and mentally squared her slender shoulders, stuck out her softly rounded chin and adopted an air of studied defiance.

Gabby muttered, 'You and whose army?'

The door looked pretty solid to her. Solid enough to withstand an earthquake. She was trapped, but for the moment safe—if you discounted her companion. Not an easy thing to do. The man was a distraction she could do without.

'Who *are* you?'

A frown of concentration on her face, Gabby glared at the door. She did not turn her head, and therefore missed the look of stark incredulity that chased across Rafiq's lean dark features when she waved a hand in impatient dismissal.

'Not now, *please*—I'm trying to think,' she

snapped. Trying, but not really getting far. And she blamed this partly on her rotten luck.

There might be times when being trapped in an enclosed space with a man who appeared to have been gifted with a dangerously generous share of pheromones was not a hardship, but this wasn't one of those times. Actually, that wasn't true. She had never been attracted to overtly macho men. She went more for the intellectual type, a man who wasn't afraid to show his emotions and his vulnerability, but such men were thin on the ground. Actually, she was unsure whether they existed outside literature and her imagination—it could be she was doomed to settle or remain single.

Rafiq was accustomed to being treated with a level of deference by virtually everybody he met. He had not been so casually dismissed since he was a boy—and then the only woman in a position to do so had been his mother. It was an irrational response to rudeness, but he found himself even more curious about the blonde.

Why not invite her for a dinner date as you have so much time to waste?

He frowned in unappreciative response to the ironic voice in his head, and allowed his glance to wander to the neatly trimmed pearly fingertips she was rubbing along the slightly tip-tilted end of her small nose. This woman was like none he had encountered in his thirty-two years. And he wasn't talking about her dress code—though it was nothing short of a miracle that she still managed to look feminine dressed like *that*!

He watched as she lifted her hand and dashed it across her face. Her hair was honey-gold, with paler shades woven in with the silky mesh that fell to her shoulders.

As his eyes slid down her body it became obvious that his curiosity was not the only thing this woman had awoken. The ache in his groin was increasingly hard to ignore. He might be dying, but nobody had told his libido, it seemed!

Gabby turned her head at the sound of his laugh, her darting blue gaze moving indignantly across his lean features. 'You think this is *funny*?'

'I think it is extraordinary that I am laughing.' Not to mention lusting.

Gabby glared, bemused by the cryptic response. 'Who are you, Gabby Barton?'

Feathery brows several shades darker than her hair twitched into a straight line above her neat nose. The intensity of his narrowed stare made her uneasy. 'Not a thief, if that's what you're thinking. I didn't come to steal the family silver.'

'I believe you,' he soothed. 'But you have a purpose…what have you come here for?'

Gabby was gripped by a sudden irrational compulsion to pour out her troubles to this total

stranger. Tell him the whole tangled tale…
Appalled that she was about to go all weak—little
woman crying on the shoulder of a big strong
man—she closed her mouth with an audible snap
and shook her head.

Of course if her problem could be solved by brute
force it might well be worth getting him on her side.
But she wasn't the type of person who off-loaded her
problems onto anyone—least of all someone she
had just met!

CHAPTER THREE

RAFIQ watched as she lowered her eyes, causing the tips of her lashes to brush against her slightly grubby cheek. She remained silent.

'A woman of mystery…'

'No mystery,' she denied, shaking her head.

'How did you get into the palace?'

'How do you know I wasn't invited?'

One black brow slanted satirically as he glanced towards the door.

Gabby's slender shoulders lifted. 'All right,' she conceded. 'I wasn't. I sort of *slipped* in.'

His brows hit his hairline. *'Slipped in?'* He shook his head in a firm negative motion. 'That isn't possible.' Incredulity deepened his voice a husky octave, and it feathered across Gabby's nerve-endings as he repeated, 'You *slipped in* past Security?'

'In the back of a delivery van.' It had been one of those moments when you acted on instinct and didn't have time to think about the consequences.

That came later, she thought bitterly, when you were trapped in a room with armed men outside the door. Not that she regretted it for a second. If she hadn't at least tried she would never have forgiven herself.

Rafiq thought about the substantial budget earmarked each year for palace security, and a muscle clenched in his lean cheek once more as he fought the unexpected desire to laugh. The girl was more than unusual, she was unique—though he had not dismissed the possibility she was mentally unbalanced just yet.

'And when it slowed down I...I got out...'

This casual confidence sent Rafiq's eyebrows in the direction of his dark hairline. 'It was moving?' He tried to imagine any of the women he knew leaping out of a moving vehicle and failed.

He felt reluctant admiration stir once more. Whoever this woman was, she did not lack courage—or for that matter recklessness. And today had taught Rafiq that when all other alternatives were exhausted *reckless* was sometimes the only thing left.

'Not very fast...' She lifted a hand to the shoulder seam of her shirt. The skin beneath was grazed and starting to bruise.

His brow furrowed in concern as he saw the specks of bright blood on the cotton. 'You are injured?'

He didn't wait for her denial. Gabby watched

with horror as he strode with purpose towards the door, his white robe billowing around his tall frame.

He was going to let them in!

She acted without thinking and threw herself between him and the door. Shrill panic threaded her voice as she caught his arm.

Their eyes met, and there was a long, still, nerve-shredding silence, Gabby's world narrowed until the only things she was conscious of were his mesmerising sloe-dark eyes and the thunderous beat of her heart as it pounded in her ears.

It was Rafiq who broke the tableau, the breath expelled from his lungs in one slow, audible hiss as his dark glance moved from her wide, beseeching eyes to the small pale hand on his arm.

Gabby saw the direction of his gaze, saw the inexplicable astonishment in his expression, but she didn't let go. If anything she clung harder, her fingers tightening into the taut, rock-hard muscle of his arm.

Her breath came in panicky gasps as she appealed with husky urgency, 'Please—don't let them in.'

Rafiq's glance flickered across the soft contours of her face. Her full lips trembled, and under the smudges of dirt the freckles across the bridge of her nose stood out against the dramatic pallor of her skin. Her electric blue eyes held the zealot-like glow of sheer desperation.

He shook his head. 'I must. You need a doctor.'

Gabby unpeeled her fingers from his arm, finding her digits strangely reluctant to respond to her commands. Mission accomplished, she absently rubbed her palm across her thigh. The impression of sinewy strength in his forearm seemed to have imprinted itself on her hand.

'It's nothing,' she promised, ripping the fabric of her shirt a little more than it already was to prove her point, revealing the smooth curve of her shoulder and the beginning of a large area of bruising in the process.

'I can't feel it,' she said, between clenched teeth.

But she could feel the brown fingertip he slid down the exposed curve. And her nervous system's reaction to a touch that was so light it barely stirred the soft invisible down on her pale skin was totally disproportionate. Every nerve-ending in her body came alive, and a heavy, creeping warm lethargy invaded her suddenly uncooperative limbs.

There was not a breath of air in the room. She doubted this sort of stillness existed outside the eye of a hurricane, where the fragile illusion of security was coloured with the anticipation of the storm that was just waiting to break.

She could feel the pressure in her eardrums as her heart-rate began to race. The air thrummed with tension—unacknowledged and almost tangible.

Gabby struggled to maintain her indifferent pose, and to control her shallow, uneven breathing as his fingertip moved upwards, tracing the angle of her collarbone in a light, feathery motion. Unable to bear the prickling heat under her skin and the dragging sensation low in her belly another second, she pulled away.

'I told you—I'm fine.' Gabby glared at him, resentment shining in her eyes as they connected with his and stayed connected. She was utterly mesmerised by the febrile glow smouldering deep in his dark eyes.

Rafiq did not speak until the heat in his blood had cooled—which meant he was silent for some time.

What he had felt when he touched her skin had been raw and primitive. It didn't take enormous powers of analytical deduction to conclude it was some form of delayed reaction, because he was not a man who allowed his passions to rule him, but it was easy to understand why some men finding themselves in his position might chose to blot out the bleak reality of their situation. They might turn to alcohol, jump in the driver's seat of a fast car or sit astride a horse and try and outrun the devils within.

And then others might bury themselves physically and mentally in the soft body of a desirable woman...

His eyes brushed the slender white column of her neck before reaching the full curve of her wide mouth. His chest lifted as he dragged in a fractured breath. *A woman like this one.*

'Do you imagine that the men outside are going to go away? Why can't you admit defeat gracefully?'

'There's nothing graceful about defeat,' she retorted scornfully.

Her apparent inability to see that she had lost irritated him. But the irritation melted into antagonism as the memory of the raw desire, the tidal swell of devouring hunger that had washed over him moments earlier surfaced.

'Not admitting you have lost does not make it any less a reality.'

Nice sermon, admitted the ironic voice in his head. *Is it intended for her or you, Rafiq?*

Gabby compressed her lips, regarding him with seething resentment. Did he think she didn't *know* that her situation was impossible? Did he think she didn't *know* she only had herself to blame?

Her lips curled into a derisive smile. '*Lost...?* I'm not playing a game.'

'You are delaying the inevitable.'

'Thank you for that pearl of wisdom,' she snapped sarcastically. 'If you want to be helpful you could go out there and tell them I'm not here...'

'Why would I lie for you?'

Gabby scowled at him. 'Maybe they don't know you're here either?'

'I imagine they will be shocked to find me present.'

The admission drew a *hah* from Gabby. 'I thought as much! You're not meant to be here either, are you?'

His lashes, jet and lustrously curled, swept downwards, concealing the satirical gleam in his dark eyes from Gabby as they brushed the slashing angle of his cheekbones.

'This room is off-limits to everyone but the Crown Prince.'

The information made her examine her surroundings with fresh interest. 'Really?' Her voice echoed her surprise. 'A sort of bolthole?' she mused.

Compared with the parts of the palace she'd seen, this was as plain as a monk's cell—a well-read monk who liked comfy chairs.

'Maybe he gets bored with the glitter? He likes books,' she added, running her finger along the spine of a thick leather-bound volume open on the table. She read the title and her eyebrows shot up. 'Not what I'd call light reading, so he's not just a pretty face.'

'You are familiar with the Prince?'

Gabby laughed and folded her arms across her chest. 'What do you think?' She rolled her eyes. 'If you must know, I read an article.'

'Was it a critical article?'

The suggestion drew a laugh from Gabby.

'Hardly! Either your Prince Rafiq has just

stepped directly off Mount Olympus, or someone paid the journalist to write nice things, or she had a massive crush on him—because *nobody* is that marvellous. Personally it made me queasy to read all that gushy stuff.'

The odd look on his face made her recall the embassy man's warning.

'The people here are very protective of their royal family, so avoid saying anything that could offend.'

'*Gushy…?* I must have missed that one.'

The admission was delivered in a flat tone, but she had the impression that far from being offended he was amused. It just showed that the embassy man had been wrong—people here did have a sense of humour.

His dark eyes scanned her face. 'I am going to open the door you know. Sooner or later.'

Gabby gave a resigned sigh, compressed her lips and nodded. Short of sprouting wings, there was no other way out, and he was right: she was delaying the inevitable. It had also crossed her mind that the longer she kept the men outside waiting the less likely they were to be sympathetic.

Sympathetic? Ever the optimist, Gabby. They'll probably fling you into a cell next to Paul.

'I suggest you stay there, be quiet, and restrain any impulses you have to do something dramatic or foolish.'

'I suppose you're going to be in trouble too…?'

She struggled to feel some genuine sympathy, but it was hard when he didn't look perturbed by his predicament, and she couldn't rid herself of the suspicion that he was the type of man who liked to break the odd rule once in a while just for the hell of it.

Under a tightly controlled surface, she decided, studying the lean hard lines of his face, he had a combustible quality. But then he was a man of contradictions. Like his mouth, she thought, her eyes straying in that direction. The stern upper lip and the full sexy lower lip, sending two opposing messages…

'I am already in trouble.'

The cryptic response made her frown. 'I'll make it clear you didn't help me or anything.'

He inclined his dark head, and something she could not interpret flickered at the back of his eyes. 'Thank you.'

'Why are you here?'

'Why are *you* here?' he shot back seamlessly.

'I was looking for someone.'

'The Crown Prince?'

'At a pinch he'd do, I suppose, but, no—not really. I need someone with more clout.' A choking sound made her tilt her head to look at him.

'I think you'll find that the Crown Prince has a little…*clout*.'

'Maybe,' she conceded, dismissing the absent

royal with a shrug, and a worried glance towards the door that was the only thing between her and total failure—maybe even imprisonment. 'But he isn't here, is he? There's just you and me.' Which sounded a lot cosier than it was. 'No insult intended, but I need someone important to hear what I have to say. Don't panic—I won't bore you with the details.'

Without the belligerence she seemed much smaller, more delicate, and the bleak note of resignation in her flat voice stirred something he refused to recognise as concern.

'I will tell you if I'm bored,' he promised.

'Nice offer.' If he meant it—which she doubted. 'I came here to see the King.'

It sounded so absurd, even to her, that Gabby wouldn't have been surprised if he had laughed. He didn't, though she was willing to bet he would look pretty incredible if he *did* laugh, or even smile, she thought, trying to imagine the lines bracketing his stern, incredibly sexy mouth relaxing. Actually, now she thought about it, it might be easier to concentrate if he didn't laugh.

'There are official channels to receive an audience with the King, if that is your plan.' He did not add that there was also a long list for those waiting to be granted an audience with his father.

'I've no time for official channels and plans,' she admitted. 'I'm kind of winging it.'

The desperation in her manner was tinged with obstinacy as she looked around the room. There *had* to be another way out. She refused to believe that her attempt to save her brother could end in such ignominious failure.

'Are you sure there isn't any other way out of here? What about the balcony?' Without waiting for a response, her urgency fuelled by another bang on the door, followed by a second volley of threats, Gabby, her eyes sparkling, rushed headlong past him and out of the open double doors.

The balcony was not large—little more than six feet in width—and the impetus of her dash sent Gabby right up to the scrolled wrought-iron railing that came up to waist-height.

As she found herself staring down at a dizzying drop, her vision blurred and the world far below spun. A mewling sound locked in her throat as she closed her eyes.

CHAPTER FOUR

RAFIQ emerged on the balcony just as Gabby loosened her grip on the rail and her body swayed forward. A violent curse was drawn from his lips as he surged forward, his fingers closing like steel bands around her upper arms as he jerked her back to safety.

Gabby's knees had gone. Head spinning, she was only vaguely conscious of her heels dragging across the floor in the moment before she found herself hauled upwards. With a sigh she leaned back into him, her heart pounding after her near escape. His arms came up around her waist, anchoring her there, drawing her closer.

'Don't worry—I'm not going to jump.' Now that the moment of sheer terror was over she was becoming a lot more conscious of other details—disturbing details, like the hot, hard imprint of his body where her spine curved into his lean length. She was tempted to stay where she was and prolong the moment. 'Thank you,' she said huskily. 'I'm not good with heights.'

'I'm disappointed. I thought nothing frightened this jumping-from-moving-vehicles action woman.'

One arm still wrapped in a supportive band across her midriff, Rafiq felt her ribcage rise as she sought to suck in a deep breath before responding huskily, but with a lot less attitude than she had shown so far.

'So sorry to be a disappointment, but we all have our weaknesses.' It seemed a good time for her to remember that her weaknesses did not usually include being attracted by obvious beefcake —even the exotic variety.

Very exotic, she thought as the clean, musky and very male scent of his body teased her quivering nostrils. Her eyelashes brushed her cheeks as her gaze fastened onto his fingers, long and tapering where they lay on her arm. A large red stone set in a thick gold band decorated one finger. If the stone had been real it would have been worth a small fortune.

Was he married?

Did he have a brood of children and an adoring doe-eyed wife who worshipped him? The images of domestic harmony that passed before her eyes made Gabby feel vaguely dissatisfied.

Was it envy? Obviously not of the woman who was married to this total stranger, but Gabby was twenty-four, and she had never even met anyone she cared enough about to have a serious relationship with—this was one area of her life where she was risk-averse.

As recently as the previous weekend Gabby had produced a jokey response when her friend Rachel had made an exasperated suggestion that she should lower the bar and maybe have a little fun.

Gabby was no prude, but she wasn't sure she wanted the 'fun' her friend was talking about—and she wasn't about to admit that she was a closet romantic. And anyway, everyone would treat her confession as a joke. She was simply not the type of girl anyone expected to admit she believed there was someone special for everyone—someone worth waiting for.

But she couldn't help but occasionally wistfully wonder if there actually *was* anyone out there for her, and she found it increasingly difficult to even imagine meeting someone she wanted to share her life with. Maybe Rachel was right? she mused. Maybe she was just making life difficult for herself…?

It could be she was doomed to stay single. Oh, well—there were worse things—things like being married to a man every woman under a hundred lusted after, she thought.

As she sucked in another tremulous breath Rafiq could feel the tremors running through her body. She felt soft, warm, scarily delicate. The man in him recognised that he was strongly attracted to her; the Prince in him knew that even had circumstances been different, even if he hadn't just been given a death sentence, a woman like this would not be for him.

There had never been any room for distraction in his life, and that went double now. His glance flickered across the top of the blonde's tousled head. There was no doubt this woman had distraction written all over her.

Her colour heightened, Gabby pulled away and walked back in to the octagonal room. She couldn't decide if her legs felt as shaky as those of a newborn colt due to her fear of heights and the accumulated stress of the last two days, or to this badly timed *visceral* reaction to a stranger.

Now, that was weird—because she had never been attracted to men like him, who projected animal magnetism. As she tilted her chin to meet his level dark gaze she was forced to acknowledge she had never actually *met* men like him before.

Her lips twisted into a wry smile. She was guessing there *were* no other men like him…

'Why do you want to speak to the King?'

Self-recrimination tautened her soft face as his question made her realise she was in danger of losing focus here.

'I really don't see why that would be any of your business.'

There was another bang on the door—loud enough to make Gabby flinch.

Without taking his eyes from Gabby's face, he nodded towards the door. 'It is possibly *his* business.'

Gabby glared at him. 'Well, if you must know I want the King to intercede. It's my brother—he's under arrest, awaiting trial.'

Gabby watched comprehension and distaste spread across his lean face. Her chin lifted. She had seen this response before, but most people attempted to conceal it. He did not.

'Your brother is the English drug-smuggler?'

Indignation sparkled in her eyes as she retorted, 'My brother is *not* a smuggler.' She saw the look of cynical contempt in the tall Arab's face and struggled to stop her eyes falling guiltily from his. 'What's the point?' she said, throwing up her hands in disgust. 'You've already made up your mind,' she accused angrily. '*Everyone* in this stupid place has already made up their minds,' she added, with an emotional quiver in her voice as she realised Paul didn't stand a chance.

The embassy man had been right—his fate was sealed.

The idea hit him like the classic bolt from the blue. He had been searching for an answer to his problems and the answer had come looking for him—or as good as.

He smiled, and his answer glared back at him with loathing.

Had he gone mad?

Admittedly on the surface it seemed a crazy, desperate idea, but sometimes you had to think outside the box—something he was famed for, though admittedly he had never ventured this far outside on previous occasions.

He'd never had to.

His thoughts raced. This girl possessed the qualities his brother was lacking: toughness, resourcefulness and a healthy lack of respect for people in authority. And loyalty was a quality you could not buy. How many people would have gone to the lengths she had for a brother? And even now, when she knew deep down it was hopeless, she refused to give up.

And he had something she needed.

Looking at the defeated slump of her slender shoulders, and at the tears sparkling on her cheeks, Rafiq felt a moment's doubt about his intentions. He quickly pushed aside the disquiet and walked towards the door. This was about the future of his country. He could not afford sentiment.

Gabby lifted her head at the sound of the lock being clicked.

With the door half open he turned back to look at her, and Gabby lifted her chin. She had not realised until this moment that she had hoped, quite irrationally, that this stranger might be on her side. Which probably made her certifiably stupid.

Gabby waited, sickly anticipating armed men appearing. When they didn't she moved towards the door, but any tentative hope she had that the coast might miraculously be clear for her to make her escape vanished when she heard the sound of deep male voices outside.

One belonged to the man who had just walked out, the other possibly to the man who had been escorting her from the premises—though it was hard to tell, because he wasn't sounding cold or dismissive now.

If anything he was sounding…well, deferential.

Gabby was still trying to make sense of this conundrum when the tall Arab reappeared. He closed the door.

Gabby noticed immediately that the air of hauteur she had noticed in his manner was now more pronounced. She folded her arms protectively across her chest as she regarded him with deep suspicion. She was missing something.

He waved a hand towards a low divan covered in tumbled silk cushions. 'Have a seat, Miss Barton.'

Gabby didn't miss the significant fact that this was not a suggestion. 'What's going on? The guard—where is—?'

'I have convinced Rashid that you offer no immediate threat to security.'

She gave a dubious shake of her head. 'And your word was enough to make him go away?'

'Perhaps I should introduce myself?' Without breaking eye contact with Gabby, he bowed fractionally at the waist and said, 'I am Prince Rafiq Al Kamil.'

The hot colour flew once again to Gabby's cheeks.

If the introduction had come from anyone else she would have thought them delusional and politely asked if they had taken their medication, but as her gaze travelled up the length of the tall figure, from his dusty feet to his gleaming dark head, she had to bite back a groan at her own stupidity.

She might have been looking for royalty, but in her own defence she hadn't been expecting to find it so literally. If she had been thinking straight she might have worked it out herself—his whole manner proclaimed that he was speaking the truth.

So this was what the end result of centuries of breeding looked like… She had to admit that even to someone who felt a natural repugnance for arranged marriages he was a pretty good advert.

A mortified flush climbed to her cheeks. *'You're* the Crown Prince?' she said, feeling stupid.

He inclined his head in regal acknowledgement and drawled sardonically, 'A poor second, I realise, to the King, but my father is at present out of the country. You don't look very pleased,' he mused, studying her flushed face and sparkling eyes. 'Is this not what you wanted? A chance to plead your brother's case at the highest level?'

Despite the fact she had what she wanted, instead of taking this heaven-sent opportunity to ingratiate herself and plead Paul's case, she remained on her feet and shouted angrily, 'Why didn't you tell me who you were?' Adding, 'And how do I know you even *are* who you say you are? You could be anyone.'

A look of astonishment chased across his lean features. 'You wish me to *prove* who I am?'

Their eyes connected, and Gabby's short burst of irrational anger subsided. She shook her head, retracting the challenge before taking the seat he had previously proffered. She would have infinitely preferred the dark wood chair beside it to this low divan that would not have looked out of place in a harem.

How did harems work?

Did *he* have one?

The questions popped unbidden into her head, and it was hard to mentally drop the theme as she watched him lower his long, lean length into the slatted designer chair she would have preferred herself. It was not exactly difficult to see him in the role of desert predator.

'Would you like some refreshment?'

She shook her head, and took a deep breath before launching into her practised impassioned plea. He didn't interrupt, even when—despite her intention to make her argument with dispassionate cool and not come across as a hysterical female— her voice became suspended by tears and she had to wipe her wet face on the hem of her shirt.

'And so,' she finished, having presented what she hoped was a compelling argument, 'my brother was foolish—really stupid,' she conceded. 'But he didn't do anything criminal. You could say he's the victim here.'

'You could. But I would not.' If the man she spoke of had been a youth, a teenager, he might have felt more sympathy, but it was incomprehensible to Rafiq that a man of thirty could be as naive as the man she described.

Gabby bit her lip. 'He made a mistake. But he doesn't deserve to go to jail for twenty-five years. If it helps, I can promise to make his life a living hell if you let him come home.'

Gabby could see no softening in his attitude as he wondered aloud, 'Does your brother appreciate what a powerful advocate he has in you, I wonder?'

Frustration robbed her retort of diplomacy. 'I'm not here to ask for favours. I'm here to demand justice. And if that doesn't work—'

He raised a brow. *'Demand?'*

'All right,' she conceded, back-pedalling. 'I'll grovel and tell you you're marvelous—even though you don't seem to have heard a word I've said.' Had anything she'd said made *any* impact on him? 'Oh, and I have these,' she added, lifting her bottom from the divan and extracting the papers she had stuffed in her back pocket. 'Character references. I'm not saying that Paul is a saint, because he isn't, and quite honestly he doesn't have the sense he was born with. But there isn't an ounce of vice or malice in him,' she promised sincerely. She smoothed the papers before extending her hand.

There was a pause before Prince Rafiq took them from her, but he made no attempt to look at them. His eyes remained directed with an intensity she found unnerving on her face.

'Aren't you going to look at them?'

'I'm sure they show your brother in a favourable light. You would hardly bring me anything that did not do so.'

Frustration bubbled up in Gabby. 'If you weren't going to take me seriously why did you let me waste my time talking?'

'Because I wanted to see how much your brother's freedom means to you.'

'Like a lab rat, you mean?' she suggested, her tone of polite enquiry at stark variance with the militant sparkle in her eyes. 'You were dangling candy?'

His eyes slid over her body and he gave a shrug. 'I can think of more flattering analogies,' he observed drily.

'Don't tell me—dog? Donkey…?' He, she thought, her eyes sweeping his face from under the protective sweep of her eyelashes, would be something lean, sleek and unpredictable… A panther, perhaps—although there was something wolfish about him now, as he bared his teeth in a smile that left his remarkable eyes cold.

Ignoring her cranky interjection, he conceded, 'I wanted to gauge what you might do to gain him a pardon.' His dark eyes narrowed as he scanned her face. His voice was soft as he asked, 'What *would* you do, Miss Barton?'

Gabby shook her head in bewilderment. 'What do you mean, *do*?'

'I mean what price do you put on your brother's freedom?'

She felt the first flicker of real hope, but remained cautious as she asked, 'Are you saying you could get Paul released?'

'I could.'

'But will you?'

The pause stretched, and Gabby held her breath. 'That is…negotiable.'

Shaking with relief, she surged to her feet. If he had been anyone else she would have kissed him. Her eyes brushed his mouth, and the image that flashed in her head sent her stomach into a roller-coaster dip.

She tried to pretend the heat rush was an air-conditioning fault rather than hormones, and trained her gaze on a relatively non-fantasy-provoking area of his anatomy. Although there was nothing aesthetically unpleasing about middle of his chest.

'I'll do anything!' she pronounced.

CHAPTER FIVE

HER unquestioning response caused Rafiq to experience an inconvenient spasm of guilt.

'This is something you should think about,' he cautioned.

He could not be fairer—there was no question of deception or taking advantage of her obvious fatigue. She could choose to walk away. He would not stop her.

Gabby frowned as he rose to his feet and stood there, towering over her. She hastily followed his example—but with a lot less towering and none of the co-ordinated animal grace that epitomised all his movements.

'I don't have to think about it. I would do anyth—' Her confident assurance was cut short by the single finger pressed to her lips. Gabby's blue eyes flew wide. The contact didn't just silence her tongue, it shut down every link between her brain and her limbs. She was literally paralysed...*with lust?*

Gabby immediately dismissed this laughable

theory. She was clearly suffering the physical symptoms of stress and exhaustion—he wasn't even her type.

Why exactly, asked the voice in her head, *do you feel the need to tell yourself that again? It's not as if you're fooling anyone,* it pointed out, *least of all him.*

Gabby's wide blue gaze lifted to the Prince's lean face. Previously she had been so mesmerised by him that she had failed to notice how deep the lines bracketing his mouth were, how tightly the smooth golden flesh was drawn across the sharp planes and angles of his face, how there was a grey tinge to his complexion.

She felt a flash of concern that vanished the moment their glances connected. This man was the very last person in the universe who needed her sympathy.

'Do not commit yourself until you know what the price is…' His finger left the cushiony softness of her pink lips and trailed lightly across her cheek before falling away.

The menace in his cryptic advice sent a shiver of fear trickling down Gabby's sweat-dampened back. She asked apprehensively, 'What do you mean, *price*?'

'Miss Barton, there is no such thing as a free lunch. Speaking of which—I will arrange refreshments.'

'No!' Gabby grabbed his arm and Rafiq turned his head.

Aware of the rapid progress of the deep flush that was working its way up her neck, Gabby dropped her hand. She resented the way that with the quirk of one flyaway black brow he could make an innocent tactile gesture seem something a lot more complicated.

'I don't want food, I want…' *I want my legs to start working, so that I can run somewhere I don't have to deal with someone with weird pewter-shot eyes making it hard to concentrate.*

Gabby was instantly ashamed of her selfish reaction. This was about Paul. This man could save him—and what was she doing? Turning accepting his hospitality into a battle of wills. It wasn't going to kill her to be civil to the man, was it?

'Nevertheless you will have lunch.'

She bit her lip. Civil was fine in theory, but did he have to present everything as a damned ultimatum?

'The decision I will ask you to make should not be made when you are suffering from exhaustion.'

'I am not exhausted.' Even as she spoke Gabby was conscious of the uncontrollable tremor in her limbs and the cotton wool sensation in her head.

'No?' He raised a brow and studied her face objectively. 'When did you last sleep? Eat?'

It wasn't until he introduced the subject that Gabby realised that it was a long time since she had done either. Once her adrenaline levels dropped she recognised she was not going to be able to negotiate her way out of a paper bag! Food was probably a good idea—and caffeine was an even better one.

'Or, for that matter, bathe?'

Gabby sucked in an offended breath. 'Are you saying I smell?'

The memory of the floral-scented female smell that had teased his nostrils when she had been in his arms came back to Rafiq, and without warning desire slammed through his body. An image formed in his mind of her, soft and warm, lying beneath him, her arms wrapped around him and her long blonde hair spread out on a pillow...

The image was so strong that he was sucked into a wild sensual vortex as the room and reality receded.

Gabby knew she was not drop-dead gorgeous, but she was vain enough to resent his pointed reminder that she looked like a wreck—especially when the comment had been made by the most spectacularly gorgeous man on the planet.

'And you're one to talk,' she snapped, studying the drawn lines of his patrician face with a speculative frown. 'When did *you* last have a decent night's sleep?' And how unfair, she reflected, her gaze lingering on the sensual upper curve of his mouth, that being sleep-deprived didn't stop him looking incredible.

Her challenging expression morphed into one of bemusement as he continued to stare at her. There was a sheen of moisture on his broad brow, and the expression in his dilated eyes was oddly blank.

'Are you all right…?'

Rafiq blinked, the effort causing beads of moisture to break out along his upper lip as he dragged himself clear of the sensual scene playing out in his head. A man who normally prided himself on his control, he was shocked to be caught displaying the restraint of a teenage schoolboy with raging hormones.

A muscle in his lean cheek clenched. 'I'm fine.'

'If you say so.' Gabby did not bother to hide her scepticism. 'But if you ask me, if anyone looks like they need a good feed it's you.'

It was not the observation that startled Rafiq but the person it came from. His weight loss had gone totally unnoticed by those close to him.

It seemed ironic that a total stranger had noticed what they had missed and he—he had ignored. If he hadn't…

He shook his head fractionally. There was no point going there. Such perception, however, would be useful for the role he had in mind for Gabby Barton.

'It doesn't matter who you are, you can only get away with burning the candle at both ends for so long,' she pointed out, oblivious to the fact that people did *not* rebuke the Crown Prince of Zantara.

'My life is one long party,' Rafiq drawled sardonically.

A party that probably involved a lot of women—the sleek, sexy sort. Well, they weren't going to be ugly, were they?

Gabby's lips formed a moue of distaste. 'You can swing from the chandeliers for all I care,' she said, with a shrug that was intended to establish her total uninterest in his social life. 'What do I know? All that inbreeding has probably bred out your need for sleep.'

That would have been convenient, Rafiq reflected, giving a hard laugh. The night sweats and insomnia and his resulting constant fatigue had been some of the collection of insidious symptoms that had made him eventually seek medical advice.

Having never suffered a day's illness in his entire life, it had not crossed his mind that the doctors would discover any sinister cause.

'Have I said something funny?'

He shook his head. 'Not funny, just insightful.'

'You mean you *don't* need sleep?'

Only too aware of how badly he needed to sleep, Rafiq ignored the question. 'Our gene pool is really not so stagnant as you appear to think. Over the years there have been many infusions of fresh blood.'

And had those infusions been willing additions to the gene pool? Gabby speculated. Or had his relations—the ones he had inherited that mouth and eyes from—ridden around the desert abducting nubile maidens who caught their fancy?

It was not exactly a big stretch to see Rafiq Al Kamil in the role of desert Sheikh, astride some high-bred stallion, his flowing desert robes flying as he scooped up another victim before riding off into the sunset with his prize and installing her in some silken tent.

Gabby had only the faintest mental image of the tent, but a very vivid representation in her head of the sleek-bodied, bold-eyed seducer of innocents as he tore off his robes.

Her waking fantasy was interrupted by his bored drawl. 'I am merely offering you hospitality. I would like you to be rested and lucid when we discuss this matter further. Do not be rash, Miss Barton, because I will hold you to any promises you make.'

Gabby didn't know if the sinister note in his warning was a creation of her fertile imagination, but after he had swept away to God knew where, without offering her even a crumb of explanation, she sat reflecting on his departing comment.

For the first time she asked herself what the price he put on her brother's freedom was. What did she have that a prince who had everything wanted?

She was sitting pondering this when her lolling head hit her chest, and she jerked upright with a cry. The last thing she wanted to do was fall asleep. She needed to keep her wits about her. Shaking her head to clear her muzzy thoughts, she got up and scrubbed her eyes with her fists. She began to pace the room.

Of all the places she could have ended up when she ran she had found herself here—was it fate?

What *could* she have that the Prince wanted?

Catching sight of her reflection as she passed a full-length mirror in a heavily carved ornate frame, she let out a groan of startled dismay.

Her hair that had started the day—or was it yesterday? She had lost track—secured at the nape of her neck in a ponytail now streamed down her back and curled in wild disarray around her face. Any trace of make-up was gone, and her face and wrecked clothes were liberally smeared with dirt from where she had landed face down in the dust when she had rolled from the delivery truck.

'Oh, Lord!' Easy to see now why the man had suggested she needed a wash!

One hand lifted to her head, she approached the mirror. Well, one thing she could rule out was him asking for sexual favours in return for Paul's freedom—not that she had ever ruled it *in*.

Remembering the paralysing stab of lust that had immobilised her when he had touched her, she just prayed he had no inkling of her mortifying reaction. God, to think she had actually imagined for a split second that it had been mutual…

Gabby grimaced at her reflection. Talk about deluded! Unless possibly the Prince had a thing for bag ladies…?

Licking her finger, she tried to rub a smear of dirt

off her cheek. Besides, even if he had been smitten with terminal lust at the sight of her—a low chuckle of self-deprecation escaped her throat at the thought—he didn't strike her as the sort of man who traded for sexual favours.

Why would he, when he had probably been fighting off women with a stick all his adult life? Or maybe *not* fighting? This possibility made her frown severely at her reflection.

Running her fingers through her hair in an attempt to tame the wild waves, she did not at first see the young woman who had appeared quietly in the room, and when she did she jumped.

'Oh—I didn't see you there.'

'Sorry, miss.' The girl bowed her veiled head. She was young and very pretty, and regarded Gabby with ill-concealed curiosity. 'The Prince has asked me to show you to your rooms.'

I have rooms? Gabby decided not to question it, though the alteration in her status from unwanted intruder to honoured guest was hard to get her head around. In a lot of ways she had felt more comfortable when they were trying to throw her out. That at least had had the feel of normality, whereas what was happening now was deeply surreal.

'Lead the way,' Gabby said, wondering what she'd let herself in for.

Gabby tried, but all her attempts at making conversation with her guide drew only a nervous laugh or a startled look from the big fawn eyes, so eventually she lapsed into awed silence.

It was hard *not* to be awed by the sheer scale and splendour of the palace—a splendour that Gabby had not had the time to appreciate during her earlier flight.

The young girl led Gabby through a maze of wide corridors and splendid ornate courtyards to an area of the palace her earlier wanderings had not led her near. Here, the splendour went up to a new level.

They turned a corner, and Gabby drew a startled breath. The wall to her left was fitted with a vast floor-to-ceiling stained glass window. Light streamed through, casting a vibrant shadow that danced on the ceiling and trickled down like liquid gold fingers onto the floor.

The girl looked around in enquiry when Gabby stopped, apparently oblivious to the breathtaking magnificence.

'It's beautiful,' Gabby said, gesturing to the glass panel.

The girl looked puzzled, but flashed Gabby a sweet smile. She gestured to a wide sweeping staircase that led to the floor above, the dozens of thin gold bangles on her wrist jangling musically.

She walked along the corridor so quickly that Gabby, whose legs felt like lead, lagged behind. At the far end she opened a door and gestured for Gabby to enter.

'Your rooms, miss.'

The sitting room alone had about three times the floor space of the entire tiny flat her parents had converted for her on the top storey of the Edwardian house where she and Paul had grown up.

Their homing pigeon, her parents called her. Gabby had never felt any impulse to travel to far exotic places. Straight out of college a job in the local primary school had come up, and she had been delighted to get it. Some people were adventurous, but she just wasn't one of them. She didn't dream about faraway places. Ironic, really, because here she was, in a place more exotic than she'd imagined existed...

She did a full three-hundred-and-sixty twirl and let out a silent whistle. 'This is incredible.'

Her guide smiled with pleasure and gestured towards the doors that were flung open onto a wide balcony.

'You would like to see the view? Many admire it. When your Prime Minister stayed his wife took many photographs.'

Gabby smiled at the girl, impressed. *Prime Minister!* 'No, thank you,' she said. She had had enough of views—and this time there would be no strong male arms to pull her back from danger.

It was a classic case of out of the frying pan into

the fire, because Rafiq Al Kamil did not represent safety except for Paul, she thought, squeezing her eyes shut and crossing her fingers as she murmured fiercely under her breath, *'Please* free Paul.'

A smile tugged the corner of her mouth as an image of her brother popped into her head. He was smiling, and then he wasn't, and then he wasn't blond and he wasn't Paul.

Gabby opened her eyes with a snap, and rubbed her upper arms vigorously to dispel the rash of goosebumps that had broken out over her skin. The cold that had made her shiver had turned her thoughts in the dangerous direction of the heat that had burned through the layers of clothing when Rafiq had hauled her back from the brink.

It seemed to Gabby that she was still on the brink—the brink of going quietly crazy. She extended her hand to push back her hair and saw she was shaking again. She felt a surge of relief. She wasn't going mad—she was just experiencing a severe blood sugar dip. She had felt like this before, when she had skipped a meal or two because she was busy.

Well, that accounted for some of it. But she had to admit missing a meal had never caused her to look at a man and feel the shameful slow burn of desire low in her belly.

She turned with an over-bright smile to the girl. 'Do you think I could have a cup of tea?'

'Your meal will be here presently. I will make sure that there is tea, miss. You will have time to bathe, if you wish, and there are fresh clothes in the bedroom.'

Gabby smiled in acknowledgement of the offer, even as she thought *no thanks*.

Once alone, she explored. She bounced on the enormous bed and pulled back the counterpane to admire the finest Egyptian cotton linen, then pressed a selection of buttons on a panel she discovered. One of them caused curtains to silently swish across the windows, and another filled the room with the sound of a blues tune that had always been one of her favourites.

She didn't have a clue how to switch it off, so she let it play. The background sound was soothing, and it actually made her feel a bit less lost. She turned up the volume, thinking she needed all the help she could get. She was so totally out of her depth. The question was, how long could she carry on treading water before she sank like a stone?

The entire suite of rooms was sumptuously furnished, but it was the bathroom that really made her eyes pop. The sight of an utterly decadent sunken bath that could have fitted an entire soccer team brought a wistful gleam to her eyes…

The girl had said there was time. What could be the harm?

She turned on the taps and struggled to recall the

title of the song now playing as she began to strip off her soiled clothes.

She took a little while to select a bath oil she liked from the vast selection on offer, before tipping in the contents of a blue crystal flagon. The room was immediately filled with the aroma of roses as the water foamed.

Gabby inhaled and smiled in anticipation as she walked down the flight of shallow steps that led into the foaming water. In the middle of all this craziness, taking a bath seemed so marvellously normal.

She actually giggled as the water begin to lap around her ankles, then waded deeper, dropping to her knees and scooping the water in both hands. She threw it over her back and shoulders, wincing a little as it touched her bruises and grazed skin.

Then with a sigh she switched off the gushing water and stretched out, resting her head on a conveniently situated padded headrest. The effect on her body was almost instant. She could actually feel the tension begin to ease from her body as if by magic. Smiling, she ducked her head under, and emerged moments later, with water streaming down her wet face. Pushing her saturated hair from her face, Gabby lay back again.

As she floated in the warm scented water a self-protective instinct kicked in, and her overtaxed brain went numb. Staring up at the elaborate gold-embellished carvings on the ceiling, Gabby didn't feel concerned when they began slipping in and out of focus. Her eyelids felt as though they had lead weights attached—so heavy that finally she had to close them.

Just for a minute…

The combination of warm water and music had the obvious effect. Her mind emptied and she slept.

Rafiq consulted his watch as he knocked on the door of the guest suite to announce his presence. It had been an hour since he'd left Gabriella Barton, and he had not wasted that time.

Considering the time factor, the file that now lay on his desk was actually quite comprehensive. What he had read about her brother suggested, rather to his surprise, that the young man might actually *be* innocent. Skimming the pages, he had seen that Paul Barton was a perfect example of arrested development.

Innocent, perhaps, but Rafiq had little sympathy. He saw nothing to admire in the hedonistic existence of those who drifted aimlessly through life, avoiding responsibility and leaving chaos in their wake, expecting other people to pick up the pieces.

He knew all the essential facts about Paul Barton. But the information on his sister—the information that actually interested him—was less complete. It was frustrating, but he could fill in the gaps later. As nothing he had read negated his plan or made it unworkable, he was pushing on regardless.

When there was no reply to his knock he stepped inside. The music system was playing some moody jazz piece he was vaguely familiar with, but the salon was empty. The food attractively laid out on a low table was untouched and cold.

'Miss Barton! Gabby!' He flicked the 'off' switch on the music system and repeated his call. When this elicited no response either, he moved to the bedroom door and knocked loudly.

When this too yielded no result, he went inside. The canopied bed was not disturbed. The only sign that the room had been entered was the neat pile of fresh clothes he had left instructions for the maid to provide, which still lay folded on a chair.

He called out again. She had to have heard him. The novelty of being ignored did not amuse him— rudeness never amused him—and her not responding was irritatingly childish.

He laid his hand palm flat on the bathroom door, and it swung inwards.

There was no indignant screech when, after the slightest of hesitations, he stepped inside. The room was filled with steam that misted the reflective surfaces, and it took Rafiq's eyes a few moments to adjust and see the woman in the bath.

He turned his head abruptly—though perhaps not as quickly as he might have. The heightened colour along the crests of his cheekbones was hidden by the fog of steam.

He stared fixedly at the wall, still seeing the image of pale limbs and a slim body that had imprinted itself on his retina. He reaction had been that of a green schoolboy catching his first sight of the naked female form. She had made no attempt to cover herself.

'Sorry, but I did call out. When you are ready I will be in the salon.'

He was approaching the door when a soft gurgling sigh from the direction of the bath made him frown. 'Miss Barton?' He turned his head, and in a flash realised that the reason she had not replied was because she was either sound asleep or unconscious.

With a curse he crossed the room and strode straight into the water. She was lying so still that for a split second he thought she wasn't breathing. When he saw the lift of her ribcage and small breasts he felt a rush of relief that was quickly replaced by anger—furious, molten anger.

Even as he called out her name he saw the ripple of water wash over her face. Sucking in a breath through clenched teeth, he bent and placed his hand under her head, lifting her face clear of the water. She stirred sleepily and muttered something unintelligible as he picked her up. It took two attempts. She weighed nothing, but even nothing, when it was wet and slippery and uncooperative, was hard to get a grip on.

As he heaved her bodily into his arms she opened her eyes and looked at him, her gaze big and blue as a summer sky. If he hadn't come in when he had those eyes might have been permanently closed—sheer carelessness could have resulted in tragedy.

It was incandescent fury that Gabby saw on his face when she opened her eyes. She instinctively recoiled from the blaze of rage, but for several seconds there was no recognition in her eyes. Her sleep-fuddled mind was a total blank. Then events of the past two days came rushing back, and all the condensed misery and emotional turmoil hit her with the force of a brick wall.

She blinked up at the dark, lean features of Rafiq Al Kamil… He was going to help Paul, but she still didn't know whether to put him in her friend or foe file… He was actually a bit big to fit in *any* file.

He was carrying her as though she weighed nothing, and there was no element of softness about him. Physically he felt all hard bone and muscle, and mentally his gaze was as unforgiving as tungsten steel.

Hold on! She blinked, frustrated at the time it was taking her brain to assimilate the most basic information. Then abruptly the time-lag between her seeing something and interpreting it narrowed, and her eyes widened to their fullest extent. He was *carrying* her!

'What are you doing?' She looked down and saw her naked body. She froze. 'And why—' her voice quivered '—am I naked?'

Gabby's eyes slowly lifted. Wild panic was triggered as they connected with his, and she was swallowed up by a tide of mind-numbing horror. She began to struggle wildly, hitting out and screaming at the top of her lungs. She landed several blows before he responded to her shrill commands to put her down!

'Be still!'

Panting from her exertion, Gabby looked at the towel held out to her with deep suspicion, before grabbing it and wrapping it around herself. Swathed from head to toe, she felt slightly more secure, but she was still shaking as she angled him a look of withering contempt, struggling to stop her teeth chattering.

She directed a narrow stare at his dark face. 'T…take another step closer…touch me and I'll…' *What?* Gabby asked herself. *Scream? Because that's done so much good so far, hasn't it?*

CHAPTER SIX

'LET me ease your mind. There is no incentive you could offer that would make me come within five feet of you.'

He had always been drawn to cool goddesses, so in theory Rafiq knew that holding a wet, screaming, squirming, volatile virago should not have aroused him.

He dug his hands deep in his pockets in a vain attempt to disguise the fact that he was in fact deeply aroused. It was a case of theory losing out yet again when it collided with reality—especially wet, slippery reality.

Her smooth brow pleated in a deep frown as she tried to follow the sequence of events that had landed her naked in his arms. 'How did I…?'

The last thing she remembered was soaking in the tub.

'I was taking a bath…' She shook her head and threw him an accusing glare. 'Do you make a habit of sneaking up on women when they're taking a bath?'

His nostrils flared. 'I did not *sneak*.'

'Well, you sure as hell didn't knock!'

'I did.'

This was getting childish—though there was nothing adolescent about his body in that suit, or presumably out of it—not that it was a subject that interested Gabby. She rolled her eyes, radiating a scorn she was far from feeling. She had lost time... how long?

Her thoughts were in a spiralling loop of bemusement. Had someone drugged her tea...? No, she hadn't had any tea. Her dry throat reminded her of that. Or was it the result of the terror she had experienced when she'd found herself naked in a desert sheikh's arms?

So he was now wearing a very western suit, and the tailor who had cut it to fit his frame must have been kissing the ground he walked on—but the desert sheikh thing still applied. It didn't matter about the wrappings or the sophisticated, urbane demeanor. Deep down this man was a total barbarian—she had every right to feel terror.

Just terror...?

Gabby evaded his dark eyes and closed down that line of thought before it got going.

'You were asleep.'

Gabby's eyes lifted. She opened her mouth to

refute the crazy claim, then closed it again. A few hazy memories came slipping back, but she ignored them and produced a disdainful sniff.

Asleep! Couldn't the lecherous rat come up with a better story? Or was it possible that in some moment of insanity brought on by stress and emotion she *had* been responsible for ending up naked in his arms?

It seemed about as likely as him being overcome by lust and going Neanderthal. This man had control—iron control that it would take a lot to snap.

'I might have dozed off for a moment,' she conceded reluctantly. 'But that doesn't give you the right to—'

'Save your life?'

This drew a laugh from Gabby. 'My hero! Save my life? Pooh!' she muttered, even as the realisation that he had seen her naked hit her again. The thought kept going around in her head, and every time it did she had to fight the urge to curl up into a mortified foetal ball and pretend this was all a dream—correction, *nightmare!*

'You could have drowned.' As he thought of how close she had been, he felt anger crowding in on him again.

About to pour scorn on this, Gabby closed her mouth with an audible click. She swallowed. 'I only closed my eyes for a minute.'

Rafiq could hear the uncertainty in her voice.

His nasty smile was to Gabby's mind unnecessarily smug.

'When I got in the tub the water was stone-cold.' His sweeping gesture drew her gaze downwards, and Gabby saw the bottoms of his beautifully tailored trousers were wet to above the knee. There were dark water stains on his shirt and jacket from where he had held her.

He had held her naked in his arms. She shook her head to dispel the image that was a distraction she did not need just now—though she knew she was going to be thinking about it later.

The colour flooded her face. 'I fell asleep…? That was… I was…'

'Stupid,' he supplied helpfully.

She bit her lip, totally mortified. 'I didn't do it on purpose.' She covered her face with her hands and groaned. 'God, this is so embarrassing.'

He looked confused by her choice of words. 'Why?'

She looked at him through her fingers. Was he dense, or what? 'Because I was…'

'Naked?' he suggested, looking amused. 'Better to be embarrassed, Gabby,' he declared, 'than dead. If it helps, I *have* seen naked women before.' None of them were imprinted on his retina, though.

'It doesn't,' she hissed, thinking of women with Hollywood gloss and perfect bodies he no doubt normally swept into his arms. She wanted badly for the floor to open up and swallow her. 'Now, if you don't mind, I'd like to get dressed.' He didn't move, so she added pointedly, 'Without an audience.'

'Of course.' He inclined his head and turned to leave her.

'And…thank you,' she called, as he stood with his hand extended towards the door.

He swung back. 'It was my pleasure.'

'That's what bothers me,' she muttered as the door closed. He must have heard her because she heard him laugh, which just about made her humiliation complete.

Gabby was tempted to put her own clothes back on, but her shirt had just about disintegrated.

'Damn,' she muttered, shaking out the dress that had been left for her. The floor-length gown unfolded with a soft swish. Her eyes widened. 'Wow!'

A dreamy expression drifted across Gabby's face as she gazed at it. Layers of the finest silk in varying shades of blue, it was just about the loveliest thing she had ever seen. She had never in her life imagined wearing anything like it.

It probably wouldn't fit.

It did.

It fitted perfectly. Gabby found herself smiling stupidly as she looked at her reflection in the full-length mirror. She swung her hips and the dress belled out from her knees, the silk swishing seductively against her skin.

'My God, I almost have a cleavage!'

Not that the illusion was going to fool the man waiting for her in the next room. He already *knew* that she wasn't exactly lushly endowed. Although she had read somewhere that when it came to the naked female form men did not demand the perfection that women imagined…

Her expression sobered abruptly and she took a step back. Paul was rotting in a prison cell and she was wondering what the Crown Prince of Zantara had thought about her naked—wondering what he would say when he saw she scrubbed up quite well. How shallow and selfish did that make her?

Not to mention delusional. An infant-school teacher from Cheshire would not even register on his radar.

She shook her head and refused to think about the heat she had seen in his eyes.

Taking a deep breath, she walked into the salon. The first thing that hit her was the smell of food— she was ravenous—and then she turned, and the second thing hit her.

Rafiq Al Kamil was sitting on one of the sofas. He rose politely to his feet when he saw her. Ineffably elegant, he radiated a confidence that was totally unaffected—an integral part of him, as was

the raw sexuality that hit an unprepared Gabby
with the impact of a physical blow.

What a time to discover a weakness for tall, dark
and brooding, Gabby thought as she struggled to
mentally shift gear. She was ashamed that she had
to struggle. Her brother's dilemma should be the
first thing on her mind—not some stranger who
had made the whole brooding hero thing his own.

He didn't speak, just stared at Gabby—who stared
back. She felt his eyes as they slid down her body,
and she lifted a self-conscious hand to the silk bodice
of the dress.

'My clothes were a write-off. This isn't really
my style, but thanks.' She lowered her eyes. What
was she doing thanking the man? It wasn't as if
he'd picked it out personally.

'It is an improvement.'

The iridescent shades of blue in the gown she
wore reflected but did not outshine the brilliance
of her blue gaze. Her skin, scrubbed clean of make-
up and dirt, was revealed as flawless and porcelain-
pale, and her hair, freshly washed and still damp,
fell down her back in soft rippling waves

'Anything would be.' She shrugged.

'That is not what I meant,' Rafiq said, as he
struggled to erase the image in his head of her in
the bathtub, her pale skin gleaming and wet. It
wasn't just his body that was weakened, it seemed,
but also his brain.

Was he going to *say* what he meant?

She noticed that his glance had dropped to the creamy vee that hinted at her cleavage, and to hide the fact her heart had started hammering she let her hair fall forward to hide the flush on her cheeks.

'It is true that what you are wearing is not suitable for travelling in the backs of delivery trucks. You appear uncomfortable...are you still embarrassed?' He sounded mildly amused by the possibility. 'Shall we agree to forget the...*incident* ever happened?'

'It was a total non-incident as far as I'm concerned,' she grunted. 'So, tell me what this is about. What do you want?' *Not your body, Gabby, so stop fantasising.*

Rafiq shook his head. 'First you must eat something.' He gestured towards the table. While she had been dressing the cold food had been removed, and fresh hot dishes were set in their place.

'I'm not hungry.' Her stomach chose that moment to growl loudly.

He looked smug and walked across and lifted the lid on one of the dishes. An aromatic spicy smell drifted across to Gabby, whose mouth immediately began to water.

'Sit.'

Gabby thought about ignoring him, but decided the rebellion was pretty pointless. The sooner she humoured him the sooner she would find out what she had to do to secure Paul's release.

'And what are *you* going to do? Watch me eat?' she asked as she sat down. If so, indigestion was assured.

'I think I will join you,' he said, gracefully lowering himself with the ease of long practice onto one of the very low divan seats around the circular table.

'How cosy—a date, almost.' She piled some food onto a plate and forked some into her mouth—it was delicious.

She swallowed and felt a large pang of guilt. She was living in the lap of luxury, albeit temporarily, and Paul was probably on a diet of bread and water.

'I don't know about you, but I can eat and talk.'

But not look at him and think straight. So she didn't. She kept her eyes trained on her plate as she adopted a brisk, business-like tone.

'They're talking about putting my brother behind bars for twenty-five years, so as far as I'm concerned no price is too steep. Stop being so damned mysterious and tell me what you want. My soul?' She laughed at the suggestion, but he didn't join in—which did not seem like a good sign to Gabby.

'What do you think of my country?'

Gabby's impatience showed as she snapped back, 'I've not actually had a lot of time for sightseeing.'

'I will call you Gabriella.'

'And what will I call *you*?' She could think of several things, but most of them would probably get her arrested for treason.

'My name,' he said, laying a hand lightly on his chest, 'is Rafiq.'

'I can't call you that!'

He looked mildly surprised by her appalled denial. 'Why not?'

Gabby, who couldn't think of a single reason beyond the uncomfortable implied intimacy of using his name, ignored the question.

'Look, why have you brought me here? What is this about? The food, the dress, the...' She stopped, suddenly realising that there wasn't a soul in the world who knew where she was. The fork stopped halfway to her mouth. She had lost her appetite. She'd practically been kidnapped and she hadn't even noticed.

'I told the man at the embassy...' She scoured her memory and triumphantly produced his name. 'I told Mr Park I would telephone him at six. If I don't he will come and collect me.'

'Really? He did not mention it when I spoke to him.'

Her eyes widened. 'You spoke to the man at the embassy? You told him I'm here?' Gabby grimaced. When she had left the bespectacled diplomat she had promised she wouldn't do anything rash. Her eyes suddenly widened 'Did you make a complaint about me?'

'I spoke to Mr *Parker*,' Rafiq confirmed. 'And I made no complaint.'

Gabby expelled a relieved sigh. She didn't want to alienate one of the few people who might be on Paul's side, even if he was hopeless.

'When I told him you were here it was news that caused him some alarm,' he informed her. 'He was under the impression that you were happy to let him act on your behalf.'

Gabby wrinkled her nose. 'Well, the man was about as much use as a wet lettuce leaf. All he could talk about were diplomatic channels and how these things take time. I couldn't wait.'

Something flickered in the back of his deepset eyes. Gabby was struggling to interpret it when he said, surprisingly, 'It so happens that I share your sense of urgency.'

She regarded him with a wary frown. 'You do?'

'I do, and for the record I am not trying to kidnap you, Gabriella.'

Mortified colour flew to her cheeks. 'I didn't say that.'

'But you thought it. The door is open.' He gestured towards the double doors. 'Or at least it will be if you decide to leave. You are quite at liberty to do so whenever you wish. There are no locks, no guards... But I feel I should remind you that it was you who sought me out—or at least my father. Which was a prime example of optimism winning out over common sense.'

Gabby gritted her teeth in frustration and didn't move. 'Are you just playing with me? Is this some sort of game for you or are you actually going to help my brother?'

'That is up to you.'

'Rafiq, what do you want?'

'You are a kindergarten teacher.'

Her feathery brows shot up. 'How on earth did you know that?' she gasped.

Ignoring the indignant question, he continued. 'And you are not emotionally entangled at present. In fact you have never been seriously involved. I find this hard to believe,' he admitted. However, if his information was accurate, it did remove one impediment that might have been an obstacle to his plan.

Of course the perfect bride for a future king would be a virgin, but even his father, who attached a great deal of importance to such things, recognised that modern morality made this desirable rather than essential.

The colour climbed to Gabby's cheeks. 'Look, where are you getting this information? How—?'

'Do not be naive, Gabby. I have used the time while you were resting to make myself familiar with your brother's case.'

She gave a sigh of relief. 'So you know he's innocent?'

'I do not know this.'

She laid down her fork and fixed him with a narrow-eyed glare. 'Well, I *do* know it.'

'Shall we leave the matter of your brother's innocence out of this discussion?'

She regarded him in disgust. 'You're not the least bit interested in justice, are you?'

'I do not make a habit of interfering with the judicial system of my country. However, in this instance I am willing to make an exception.'

Gabby's lip curled. 'Yes, you're an opportunist—I get that,' she inserted impatiently. 'But what do you *want*?'

She saw the jolt of shock that stiffened his body at her less than deferential attitude. Sticking out her chin, she folded her arms across her chest and met his dark implacable gaze. She wasn't going to pretend a respect she didn't feel.

'You want your brother released from prison, his name cleared and the slate wiped clean. I want *my* brother married.'

Gabby struggled and failed to make the connection between the two. She shook her head and pushed away a silky skein of fair hair that had drifted across her face.

'What does that have to do with me?'

'I will help you achieve your objective if you help me achieve mine, Miss Barton.'

'But how can I help? Do you want me to talk to your brother's girlfriend?'

'My brother does not have a girlfriend. Well, actually he has several, but none would make a suitable consort for the future King of Zantara.'

Gabby was struggling to follow, but immediately identified a discrepancy. 'But aren't *you* the future King?'

He appeared to tense, but ignored the question and successfully diverted her attention by declaring, 'I have decided that *you* would be a suitable bride for my brother.'

Gabby blinked. 'Is that meant to be some sort of twisted joke? My God, you never had any intention of helping Paul, did you?' Throwing him a look of disgust, she folded her napkin with slow deliberation and got to her feet. 'What do you and your friends do for after-dinner entertainment? Watch traffic accidents?'

Rafiq rose to his feet and stood there towering over her. 'You asked me about the succession. You are correct. I am next in line, but I will not be King, Miss Barton.'

An expression of overt suspicion in her narrowed eyes, she folded her arms across her chest. What was this? she wondered. Another example of his warped sense of humour?

'Why not?'

A man born to be King, he looked the part—which was pretty rare in royal circles. He was regal down to his fingertips, and on the evidence so far he'd have no major problem with the ordering-people-around element of the job.

Before she had finished reflecting on his princely attributes, he had covered the space between them in two easy strides. Planting a hand on the wall behind her head, he leaned over her.

His sheer physical presence was incredibly intimidating, but Gabby was determined not to give him the satisfaction of showing him how painfully aware of him she was.

'I need your word that what I am about to tell you will not leave this room.'

The intensity of his manner unnerved Gabby even more.

'Or what?' she squeaked.

He arched a brow and gave her a look of mock surprise. 'You are in a position to threaten me?'

Gabby, who was in a position to fall in a shaking heap at his feet, shook her head and gulped. Barely audibly, she forced her response past her frozen vocal cords.

'No.'

'I *am* next in line of succession. My father was not young when I was born, and five years ago he had two heart attacks. The second was fairly major and he had surgery. He could live for a long time or he might not.'

Gabby was unsure how to respond to this information. She ducked under his arm and put some distance between them. 'The same could be said of everyone.'

'Not of me.'

'Why? Are you going to live for ever?' She gave a scornful laugh and began to turn.

'I am dying, Gabby.'

CHAPTER SEVEN

His words made her swing back. 'You're sick, all right—sick in the sense of humour department.' She pointed at her face. 'Does it look like I'm laughing?' She stopped.

He wasn't laughing either. Conscious of a knot of something close to panic building in her chest, she scanned his face, her unease growing.

'My God!' The colour drained from her face and her hand came up to cover her trembling lips. 'You're telling the truth!'

'I have perhaps six months to live. I have that time to prepare my brother for the role which will be his.'

Gabby shook her head in a negative motion and staggered backwards, until the back of her knees hit a chair. She slid into it. 'But there must be something?'

'No.' His closed expression made it clear that he found the subject uncomfortable.

'But you're young and fit...' she protested, her

eyes travelling the long, lean length of him. She had never actually seen anyone who looked more alive.

'This is not something we need to discuss. The facts are clear—not to accept them would lack… dignity.'

She was utterly bemused by his attitude. *'Dignity?'*

'There is nothing that can be done.'

She felt something snap inside her. Suddenly Gabby was so angry that for several heartbeats she couldn't speak. 'How can you be so calm about it?'

Rafiq shrugged in response and looked visibly taken aback by her reaction. 'Why should it matter to you? We are strangers.'

The question and the shrug fanned the flames of the anger that held her in its grip. Hands on the arms of the chair, Gabby pulled herself to her feet.

She tilted her head back to look into his dark, impassive face, and as she studied the strong, cleanly sculpted lines and planes of his symmetrical features she thought, He *can't* be dying! It simply wasn't possible. It had to be a mistake. She had never seen anyone look *less* weak or *more* invulnerable.

Vitality seeped from every gorgeous pore—or was that nervous energy? she wondered, the indentation between her bows deepening as her glance lingered on the dark smudges beneath his spectacular eyes.

'There *must* be something—'

He cut her off with a flat, 'There is not.' Looking irritated by her insistence, he added with horrid finality, 'I *am* dying.'

Their eyes met, and her hand went to her mouth as a tiny cry was wrenched from her throat. 'But you *can't* be ill. You don't *look* ill,' Even as she spoke she was seeing the shadows under his eyes, the lines of strain bracketing his mouth.

'I do not at present feel ill.' The doctor had explained that this was the reason why so many people who presented with this disease were already beyond treatment. The onset was insidious, and the symptoms were often limited to general fatigue, night sweats, and weight loss—not specific.

'But that's a good sign, isn't it? They are making advances in medical science every day of the week. Things that once seemed impossible—'

A muscle clenched in his jaw. 'There is nothing that can be done beyond the occasional blood transfusion as a short-term fix later on, when my energy levels drop.'

'How can you accept it this way?' she reproached him incredulously. She looked at him—tall, vital-looking, the embodiment of masculine vigour—and shook her head in utter rejection.

Rafiq's lashes dipped to hide the emotion that flared hotly in his hooded eyes. A nerve clenched in his jaw. *Accept?* Did she imagine he had any choice? Did she imagine he would not have preferred to yell and bellow?

He could not allow himself the indulgence. He needed to focus and do what had to be done for his country. His chest lifted as he expelled a deep breath and subdued the sudden irrational impulse he had to shake her or kiss her or both.

'It is a path we are all on, Gabriella.'

'Spare me the homespun philosophy, please,' she begged, rolling her eyes. In the grip of emotions she didn't even recognise, she was barely conscious that she had laid her hands flat against his chest. 'I don't call it brave—I call it defeatist and pathetic. Aren't you angry? God, if it was me I'd be *furious*!'

Rafiq lifted his eyes from the small hands that lay against his chest. 'You *appear* to be furious.'

His impassive manner further ignited her passion. 'I am,' she gritted.

'There is little point railing against fate.'

'I'm not mad at fate, I'm mad with you!' she exploded. 'You're just so, so…*passive*. It's feeble! You should be fighting! You're acting like you're dead already! But you're not.' Flexing the fingers pressed against his chest, she fixed him with a fierce sapphire stare. 'I can feel your heart beating…' She began to beat out the tattoo of the steady thud in his chest.

There was no conscious thought behind her action as she reached up impulsively, grabbing his head in her hands and dragging it down to her. Her eyes squeezed tight shut as she pressed her trembling lips to his warm firm mouth and kissed him hard. She felt a shudder pass through him, but he made no attempt to return the pressure.

She pulled clear after a moment. This wasn't about kissing him, or even wanting him to kiss her back, she told herself. It was about proving a point. The method was crude, and heavy on the drama, but she had done it.

She fixed him with a shimmering blue stare and shook her head, pressing a hand to her heaving bosom.

'*Now* do you believe you're alive?'

'You make an argument forcibly, Gabriella,' he observed thickly.

There was nothing forcible about the pressure of his mouth as it covered hers. Soft and seductive, his lips moved sensuously over hers. As his tongue traced the soft trembling outline they parted. He accepted the mute invitation and his tongue slid deep into her mouth. She felt the groan in his chest as his big hands moved to her waist and dragged her up hard against him.

The erotic pressure of his erection as it pressed into her soft belly made Gabby weak with wild desire. Her hips moved against him instinctively as she met the deep, stabbing incursions of his tongue with her own, hesitantly at first, and then with more confidence and urgency.

Then it stopped.

He put her away from him so abruptly that Gabby almost fell over. Her head spinning, she blinked up at him, waiting for the world to slide back into focus. You couldn't kiss a person that way and then act as though nothing had happened!

But he was. Could a man really turn it off that quickly? Other than the dark colour scoring his cheekbones there was nothing in his manner to suggest that moments earlier he had been fully aroused.

Maybe he still was? It was only by exerting every ounce of the will-power at her disposal that Gabby stopped her glance dropping. Unfortunately the blush she had no control over.

'A man has the right to face his death however he wishes, Gabriella.'

'Your rights! What about my rights?' Gabby, still shaking after the sensual invasion, shook her spinning head. 'It's not my *wish* to marry your brother. Or to be kissed by you,' she lied.

'That will not happen again,' he said with a formal inclination of his head. 'As delightful as the diversion was.'

In order to make true his promise Rafiq knew he would have to take care to keep her literally at arm's length in future. For some reason his brain ceased to function around her.

He was still shocked to the core that for the first time in his life he had permitted carnal need to overrule common sense and logic.

'I think we should focus on the matter in hand. It *is* your wish to save your brother from a life behind bars?'

She gave an incredulous snort. 'You were serious? You're saying that if I agree to marry your brother the charges against Paul will go away?'

'In essence, yes.'

'You want me to marry your brother. So what was that?' Her hand went to her lips. They still felt swollen and over-sensitive. 'A test run?' she suggested bitterly. 'The royal bedroom test? Did I pass?'

Gabby took an involuntary step back as fury flashed in his eyes, the pewter flecks disappearing as they darkened.

'That was a mistake,' he gritted through clenched teeth.

Mistake! This man was a master of understatement. 'On that at least we are in total agreement.'

'We will discuss it no more.'

Gabby, who hadn't planned to discuss it all, stuck out her chin and tried to match his nonchalant uninterest in the subject. 'Fine by me.'

'I appreciate this is not a decision you can take lightly, and I would like to be able to give you more time, but the fact is time is the one luxury I do not have.'

Her anger fell away, to be replaced by the cold chill of dread. 'Don't say that,' she begged in a stricken whisper.

This was the point where Rafiq could no longer pretend he was not playing dirty, so he stifled his natural sense of fair play and said, 'When you are making your decision remember that although obviously I cannot anticipate the judicial process…'

The blatant hypocrisy made her smile ironically. If he wasn't the law then he was definitely above it. 'Of course not,' she drawled.

'It seems likely, given the zero tolerance stance we take on drugs, that your brother will spend the next twenty to twenty-five years behind bars.'

Gabby's air of moral superiority evaporated. Her stomach churned sickly as an image of her sibling spending all those years incarcerated for a crime he didn't commit rose up before her.

'You're actually asking me to…?' She stopped and angled a bewildered look at his face. 'But why me?' She shook her head. 'I'm not exactly queen material. I'm sure you have a little black book filled with high-born virgins who would stab each other in the back to wear a crown.'

'Things have moved on since the little black book.'

'You're computerised? How progressive,' she

drawled sarcastically. 'Then go open a file and look for another sacrificial lamb.'

'If *you* decide to make the *sacrifice* you would be spending the next twenty-five years living in some luxury. You would be respected, and you would have a position of power and influence that most people can only dream of.'

'I have never dreamt of power and influence.'

His perfect mouth twisted into an ironic smile. 'Think about it now,' he suggested.

'What about your brother? Doesn't he have a say?'

His nonplussed expression drew a frustrated groan of impatience from Gabby.

'What,' she asked, spelling it out slowly, 'if he doesn't want to marry me? He might hate me on sight. You cannot make him marry me,' she added, when there was no corresponding glimmer of recognition in his unblinking regard. 'Unless you plan to blackmail him too?'

'My brother has lived the lifestyle of a playboy but he is aware of his responsibilities.'

'So you *do* plan to blackmail him?'

His bared his teeth in a white wolfish grin that to Gabby seemed utterly ruthless.

'I am hoping it will not be necessary.'

'Because he'll take one look at me and fall passionately in love?'

Instead of laughing, he swept his eyes from her feet to the top of her silky head.

'It is a possibility.' One that ought to fill him if not with joy then certainly satisfaction. But instead Rafiq was conscious of a vague sense of discontent.

Her lips twisted into a grimace. 'Right!' Now she *knew* he was being sarcastic, and his fixed, unblinking regard began to make her feel uncomfortable.

'You should not bite your nails.'

'I do not—' She stopped and realised that her finger was in her mouth. 'See—I'm a social liability.'

'I'm sure you can be very charming when you want to be.' The idea of her being charming to his brother caused Rafiq's vague discontent to escalate into strong displeasure.

'My brother, Gabriella, is not only a much nicer person than me—'

'Not exactly a big ask.'

'—he is quite…malleable.'

'You mean if you tell him to marry me he will?'

'I would not be that unsubtle. And I think you underestimate yourself…' he chided.

'You do know you have the moral scruples of a snake, don't you?'

His taunting smile died, and the expression that replaced it was implacable. 'I have no time for scruples, Gabriella. You and I, we both understand what few do in this world.'

'What is that?'

'Duty. How many sisters would have done what you have to save their brother from the consequences of his own foolish actions? You are a woman of resources, resolve and inner strength. You could never marry a man who is strong.'

'You mean a man like you?'

He looked startled by the suggestion. 'You and I?' he echoed, his eyes slowly tracing the wilful curve of her full upper lip. He released a scornful laugh and shook his head. 'It would be a total disaster.'

While his incredulous response irritated her, Gabby could not disagree with his scathing analysis. 'It would be a head-on collision,' she said, thinking of that kiss. That had been quite a collision.

'The modern way is to speak of marriage as a partnerships of equals.'

'And it isn't?' Gabby prompted, thinking that everything he was saying showed that at heart the 'modernising' Prince was nothing but a barbarian.

'One partner needs to take the lead.'

'You mean a leader and a follower?' No prizes for guessing which one he would be, but she wasn't exactly flattered that he tarred her with the same brush.

'I mean someone who is capable of making decisions and living with the consequences— someone who is capable of putting duty ahead of their personal desires and needs.'

Despite herself Gabby was fascinated by this insight into his belief system. 'Is that what you've done?' What, she wondered, were the desires this man had denied for the sake of duty? A woman?

She shook her head and gave a hard laugh. 'Sorry—stupid question. It's what you're still doing. You don't have a clue what I'm talking about, do you?' she added studying his face. 'Most people who knew they only had weeks to live would want to cram all the things they wanted to do but never had an opportunity to into that space of time.'

'I have led a privileged life and enjoyed opportunities beyond those that most people can dream of.'

She knew her heart ought to be aching for herself, for the choice he was forcing her to make, but instead she felt that irrational organ ache for him.

'The sort of life that you want me to embrace?' she suggested, tears thickening her voice to a husky whisper as helplessness swelled like a lump of lead in her chest.

Rafiq refused to acknowledge the misery in her voice, and reminded himself he was offering her a life that many would envy. His first duty was to secure the future and security of his country.

'It is your choice.'

Anger like blue flame flared in her eyes as she shook her head emphatically from side to side, fixing him with a sparkling sapphire stare.

'You know I don't have any choice.'

Rafiq refused to acknowledge the surge of guilt he felt as their eyes connected. 'There is always a choice, Gabriella. I am not forcing you to do anything.' It might be wise if he kept not just a physical distance between them but an emotional one too. Empathy could cause problems.

'Amazing, isn't it? But I'm not mad about this entire sacrificial lamb thing. I'm not thanking my lucky stars I met you either. But why are you even wasting your time with this obsession?'

'You call it obsession and I call it duty, Gabriella.'

She threw up her hands and covered her ears. 'Will you stop calling me that?' she yelled.

'Is it not your name?'

'Not the way you say it! *Gabriella!*' she spat in disgust, trying and failing to imitate his rich, resonant tone. 'I'm Gabby—plain Gabby. Not Queen of the May or Queen of anywhere else. When I marry I don't want to be some man's keeper.'

He quirked a dark brow. 'You have some fantasy of being dominated?'

The suggestion caused angry colour to rush to her face—or was that anger more closely connected with the graphic erotic mental image she blinked so hard to clear?

'No, I have some *fantasy* of being loved and cherished!' she yelled back, her voice shaking with the strength of her feelings. Despite that brief mental lapse, she had never had fantasies about lying naked beneath a man with a body that gleamed like oiled silk.

If she hadn't known he was totally incapable of it, she might have called the flicker of emotion that crossed his face guilt.

'My brother is a basically good man.'

'If he's nothing like you that's a head start,' she agreed, keeping her emotions and her imagination in check as she regarded him with cold disdain. 'So what's the plan? Are you going to use blackmail with him too?' she wondered, pretending great interest as she watched his lean face darken with annoyance. 'Are you going to play the "dying wish" card?'

The moment the words left her lips she wished them unsaid, and when she saw him flinch she felt even worse.

As she struggled to cling to her antagonism her stomach took a sickly lurching dive in utter rejection of the thought of this vital man being prematurely robbed of his life. Gabby had never met anyone who embodied life and vitality more. It was impossible for her to look at him and believe that he was dying.

Tears welled in Gabby's eyes and began to roll down her cheeks as she bit her lip.

Misinterpreting her silent misery, his undertaking to keep his distance forgotten, Rafiq started forward, his hand extended.

Gabby blew her nose and backed away, fending him off with one hand.

'I really don't want a shoulder to cry on—least of all yours,' she spat. 'Let's face it—you're not sorry. If any of your remorse or sympathy was genuine—if you gave a damn for anything but your duty and your country—you wouldn't be doing this… Oh, and have a I mentioned it is a totally crazy idea?'

'We are both in a position we don't want to be, Gabriella. I ask this: meet my brother. He is at present out of the country, but I expect him back in two days' time.'

She regarded him warily. 'Just meet?'

'Think of it as a first date.'

'But you expect there to be a second?'

'It is no secret, Gabriella. I have made it clear what my wishes are. My brother needs support; you are a strong, resourceful woman.'

If she really was as resourceful as he imagined she would be able to think of another way to gain Paul's freedom. 'And you'll let Paul go home?'

He nodded. 'There are formalities to be—'

'How long?' she cut in.

'Thirty-six, forty-eight hours…and then he will be on a plane back to England.'

Gabby released a shuddering breath. The sooner the better, as far as she was concerned—before Rafiq woke up to the insanity of his scheme. And she had no doubt he would. This was just his way of trying to cope with what was happening to him. Playing along and humouring him felt almost like cheating.

'I'll meet your brother.'

She could tell from his satisfied smile that he had never doubted her agreement.

'Fine. Until then I suggest we put the time at our disposal to good use.' His dark gaze drifted down her body, and he felt the lustful kick of his libido. Had the circumstances been different, that 'good use' would have involved a bed.

He inhaled and reminded himself that circumstances were *not* different, and it was *not* a good idea for a man to undress—even mentally—the woman destined to be his brother's bride.

'What sort of good use?'

Her frown, he reflected, would have been even more suspicious had she known of the carnal mental images he struggled to banish from his head.

'There are things about my country—the formalities that a princess must—'

Her jaw dropped. 'You want me to learn which fork to use?'

Her interruption brought an impatient frown to his face. 'There are customs, ceremonies…'

She rolled her eyes. 'I suddenly feel like Eliza Doolittle.'

His heavy-lidded eyes narrowed at her flippant insertion. 'One of the first things you might like to learn is that it is not generally considered good manners to interrupt a member of the royal family. I will see you tomorrow.'

'I can hardly wait.'

The worrying part was that her sarcastic parting shot as he left the room had an element of truth to it.

She had clearly lost her mind.

CHAPTER EIGHT

GABBY did not actually see Rafiq until almost the following afternoon.

Her morning had been spent with someone called Sayed. She had no idea what his specific role was in the royal household—he had introduced himself simply as a member of the Prince's personal staff—but it was clear from the level of respect given him by others that he was a man of some influence.

Sayed had given her a tour of the palace—or at least as much as could be covered in a morning. It was impossible to tell from the man's manner towards her what he had been told about her, if anything. He was obviously too polite to express anything as vulgar as curiosity.

They had now reached the library—a room of such dazzling magnificence that even after all the splendour she had been exposed to that morning Gabby was stunned into awed silence. Then Rafiq finally appeared, and Gabby was struck dumb with awe for the second time.

She watched as he walked up the wooden steps that led to the upper mezzanine level of the room. Her breath snagged in her throat.

The man really was magnificent!

Her gaze swept in an arc from his toes to his dark bare head. He was wearing what seemed to be the norm for him—riding breeches, boots, and a white flowing desert robe, above which his burnished skin glowed golden. She gave her head a tiny shake of denial, still unable to reconcile his vitality with what she knew of his illness.

He nodded quite curtly to her, and then turned to Sayed.

The two men spoke in their own tongue for several minutes, and Gabby was left to twiddle her thumbs before the older man bowed low to her and excused himself.

Gabby turned to the tall Prince. 'So what's next?' she asked arching a brow. 'Cutlery lessons?'

'I will assess the need for those at lunch.'

Gabby's wrathful glare met his steady, sardonic gaze, and her expression melted into a reluctant grin. 'If you're serious,' she warned, 'I will slurp my soup.'

His dry response disconcerted her. 'I sense you will be a charming dinner companion.'

The humour in his eyes disconcerted her some more—and she struggled not to respond to his dry humour. 'Dinner and lunch?' she said, trying not to analyse her quickened heart-rate too closely. 'I do feel honoured.'

'I would have been here earlier, but a problem required by attention. I hope Sayed was an adequate deputy.'

'He was a preferable deputy.' He hadn't shaken loose odd, uncomfortable feelings inside her. 'In-finitely preferable,' she added, dragging her eyes from his mouth. 'How did you explain to him…?'

He shook his head and looked baffled. 'Explain?'

Gabby laid a hand flat on her chest. 'Me! How did you explain me being here?'

There was no answering flicker of comprehen-sion in his face as he placed his hand on the back of a leather chair. Gabby's eyes were drawn to the dark red ring on his finger. He had lovely hands… strong and sensitive…and…

'Why would I explain anything?'

Gabby's eyes lifted to his face. Her distracted study of his hands had brought a flush to her cheeks. It remained there as she studied his lean, patrician features.

After a few seconds she laughed. 'Sorry— silly question.'

'Sayed tells me that you have asked a good many intelligent questions.'

'He does?' Gabby doused her smile and frowned, because she didn't want to make it seem as if she was eager to please. 'It was the novelty of receiving straight answers,' she observed crankily.

'I will try to be direct.' He extended his arm in invitation. 'Would you like to have lunch?'

Gabby gave a take-it-or-leave-it shrug and turned in the direction he indicated. As she did so she came face to face with a portrait that had caught her attention when she had first walked into the library. This close, the subject's beauty was even more startling.

'Her eyes really do follow you,' she murmured, studying the dark-haired beauty. Her skin seemed to glow and her eyes were as blue as the string of sapphires that hung around her slender throat. 'Who is she—or *was* she?'

'Was. Queen Sadira.'

Gabby's eyes left the painting as she tilted her head up to Rafiq. She found he was looking at her and not the portrait. 'Your mother?'

'No, she was my father's first wife. She was the love of his life.'

Gabby, who wasn't sure she would have enjoyed having the love of her husband's life looking down at her from such a prominent position, turned back to the portrait.

'But he loved your mother too?'

'No. I think he was fond of her, and he respected her, but a man only experiences that sort of... insanity once in his life.'

Gabby turned her head and found Rafiq was standing closer. She tilted her head further back and felt her stomach dip in reaction to the masculine aura he generated.

'He didn't love her?' His pragmatic observation shocked her.

'You sound scandalised,' he observed. 'You do not need to be. Not on my mother's behalf. She did not love my father—not in the romantic sense—but she respected him, and they shared a vision of what this country should be, and a strong sense of commitment and duty.'

Things, Gabby thought, studying his dark face, they had passed on to one of their sons at least. A son who even when he was dying did not think about it in personal terms but in terms of how it would affect the future of his damned country... She was conscious of anger building inside her. No one had ever given him the choice!

Why should Rafiq be expected to make such a sacrifice?

'My parents' marriage was a successful union.' Annoyance flickered across Rafiq's face as he heard the defensive note in his own voice. 'When they married the country was in turmoil. My mother was instrumental in supporting my father when he undid the years of neglect following Sadira's death.'

'You think love is a form of insanity?' She

studied his profile, her glance lingering on the passionate curve of his mouth, and wondered if Rafiq had ever known that insanity.

His eyes slid to the portrait. 'When Sadira could not bear children my father was expected to put her aside. He refused, even though the lack of a clear heir to the throne was creating major divisions.'

Gabby's tender heart bled for the tragic Queen. 'You think he should have put her aside?'

He shrugged. 'My father put his personal happiness ahead of his duty.'

'Is that a yes or a no?' It was a silly question. It was clear from his actions that Rafiq put his individual desires and needs below his duty and his country— duty had been bred into him, and he had never been allowed to be a carefree little boy or a reckless young man. He had always been the future King.

'The job of King comes with responsibilities.'

'The poor woman. She was so beautiful…' Even though her glance had drifted back to the portrait Gabby remained painfully conscious of the man beside her, and her empathy went bone-deep. 'And her eyes are incredible…so blue.'

'Not as blue as yours.'

The husky retort brought her swinging back to face him. As their eyes connected the air around them seemed to shimmer with the intensity of unspoken desires and emotions.

The only sounds in the massive room came from the mingled tick of a selection of antique time pieces and their breathing—hard to distinguish each from the other.

Gabby's stomach quivered, and her heart thundered as she struggled to breathe. Her feet seemed glued to the floor with lustful longing. She struggled to break free of the bonds of the sexual thrall that held her tight in its grip… Rafiq's eyes were so…*hot*… Oh, help!

'I… I… I'm hungry. For food,' she added, her face crimson with embarrassment.

Rafiq inhaled, his flared nostrils quivering as he scented her perfume. 'I too am *hungry*…' Ravenous described better the desire pounding through his veins.

He moved abruptly, and broke the tableau a split second before Sayed announced his return with a tentative knock.

'What is it, Sayed?' He assumed a neutral expression. She was a sensual banquet, but not his.

Standing in the vault of the room, Sayed raised his voice to reach the mezzanine level. 'I am afraid that there has been a landslip in Bahu.'

Gabby saw Rafiq stiffen as the two men continued their interchange in rapid Arabic. It didn't take an ability to understand the language to see that the situation they were discussing was serious.

Halfway to convincing herself that the entire

sizzling moment had only existed in her head, Gabby was sure of it when Rafiq turned back to her, with no residual trace of warmth in his sombre manner.

'I am needed. I must leave you.'

'Take me with you,' she heard herself say. 'That is…'

'All right,' he said, telling himself that it was a good thing if she saw some of his country and fell under its spell.

It was not a good moment to think of spells.

Conversation was not possible due to the noise during the helicopter flight. It took them three quarters of an hour, but for Gabby, staring down at the fascinating and constantly changing scenery of this geographically diverse country, the time went quickly.

Gabby wrapped the silk scarf she had been given around her head as she stepped out into the sun. She shaded her eyes and stared.

A group of black tents were scattered around a green oasis, but what dominated the site was the towering ancient stone wall rising up behind them.

Rafiq watched her jaw drop.

'It is the remains of a Crusader castle. Like the Bedouin, the Crusaders were attracted by the water, and due to the height nobody—enemy or friend—can arrive unseen.'

It was clear from the small group who came to greet them that Rafiq fell into the latter category.

'There are no men.' Gabby voiced her observation out loud.

'The men are all helping in the rescue. My father gave permission for an archaeological dig to go ahead down in the valley.'

'That's where the landslip is?'

Rafiq nodded, his expression sombre. 'Yes, several young men from here were working on the site.'

'There are injuries?'

'It appears so. The rescue is being made more difficult by sheer inaccessibility. The overhanging cliffs make helicopter access impossible, and the track is too rough for four-wheel drives. That just leaves…' He nodded towards a distant dust cloud that as Gabby watched became a group of horsemen, approaching at great speed.

She felt her stomach lurch as she saw the spare horse they were leading.

'You're going in?'

He nodded, and looked surprised by the question. 'Of course.'

'Can I come with you?'

He shook his head, something close to tenderness flickering across his face as he looked at her. Gabby's stomach flipped.

'Not this time,' he said. His expression grew troubled as he focused on her face. Then, as he hooked a thumb under her chin and tilted her face up to his, it hardened into one of self-recrimination. 'I should not have brought you.'

'What if when you go with them—?' She nodded towards the men who had reined in their mounts close by. 'What if—' she repeated, unable to keep the anxiety from her voice. 'What if you get ill?'

'I won't.'

Not a very practical response, but one that seemed to Gabby very typical of this man—this very hands-on Prince, who took responsibility a lot more literally than most.

'The women will look after you.' Rafiq had turned away to speak to the group from the tents, varied in age and all looking visibly comforted by what Rafiq said to them.

He only looked back once as he strode out to the waiting men and vaulted with lithe ease into the saddle of the spare horse. Gabby watched until the riders were nothing more than specks in the shimmering desert landscape.

The women did look after Gabby, but as they spoke no English and she spoke no Arabic, communication was limited. Her anxiety levels were rising, and she had almost chewed her nails off. When the braziers were lit, sending clouds of smoke into the darkening sky, still there was no sign of Rafiq.

She had tried several ways to ask the women when they thought Rafiq might be back, but the mention of his name had produced many giggles and smiles that were pretty much the same in any language.

Dawn was breaking when Gabby curled up on a rug beside one of the open camp fires, finally succumbing to exhaustion. But that exhaustion paled into insignificance beside the pallor of fatigue in the grime-streaked face of the man she saw when she awoke a couple of hours later.

'Rafiq!'

He stretched his long legs in front of him and hooked one ankle over the other, looking at her over the rim of his coffee cup.

'Good morning. I am sorry you were left for so long.'

Dismissing the apology with a wave of her hand, Gabby pushed aside the blanket someone had placed over her while she slept and shot into a sitting position, wincing as her cramped limbs complained.

'You should have woken me. How long have you been sitting there? You're hurt?' she asked, as her horrified gaze fastened on the blood seeping from a gash on his wide forehead.

'I am fine.'

From the way he said it Gabby knew the same could not be said of everyone. 'Were many hurt?' she asked quietly.

'One fatality,' he said, placing his cup down on a level stone with an exaggerated care that did not quite hide the tremor in his hand. He thought of the boy who had died in his arms. Later he must speak to the mother who had lost her son. 'Twenty injuries. Five of those are critical; one man lost an arm.'

She watched as he passed a hand across his eyes. The need to wrap her arms around him and offer the comfort that would obviously be rejected was so intense that it took every ounce of her self-control to stay put. She could feel his pain in her bones.

'I'm sorry.' This was a prince, she realised, who took duty to a very personal level. He really *cared*.

He flicked her a half-smile that was very white in his grime-streaked face. 'They have been air-lifted out now. A helicopter will be back for you presently.'

'You're not coming?'

He shook his head. 'I must stay.'

She didn't even try and persuade him other-wise. It was obvious that he wasn't going to change his mind.

'What about my princess lessons?'

Rafiq felt something move and twist inside his chest as he looked at her, her hair a wild halo, the dark smudges under her eyes making them seem huge. Swallowing, he shook his head. 'I think you have had a baptism of fire into our culture, so we will skip the cutlery lesson.'

'Did I pass?'

He looked at her in silence for a moment, then rose to his feet. 'Yes, you passed.'

CHAPTER NINE

PAUL'S good-looking face lit up when he saw her. He rushed forward and enfolded Gabby in a bear-like hug, before sweeping her off her feet and twirling her around in a circle.

'Put me down, you idiot,' she begged, laughing. 'Thank you,' she said, smoothing down her hair which, thanks to the ministrations of a hairdresser who must be famous because he only had one name, hung like a smooth silky curtain down to her waist.

'Thank me?' Paul shook his head. 'I don't think so. Thank *you*.' He shook his head in admiration. 'I don't know how you did it, sis—but, thanks.'

Her eyes slid from his. 'I didn't do anything,' she protested. She had wondered whether to tell Paul the truth, but had decided on balance not to. It would be pointless. Why make him feel guilty? Always supposing he actually took her seriously.

'That's not what the Parker guy said. He said you were Wonder Woman.'

'No, he didn't.'

'No,' Paul agreed, checking out his reflection in the mirror. 'I might keep the beard,' he mused, rubbing his hand against the sparse, patchy growth on his lower face. He appealed to Gabby. 'What do you think?'

'I think no.'

Paul sighed. 'You're probably right. The chicks don't dig facial hair,' he added with a mock leer.

'Must you use that word?' she asked with distaste.

'While it annoys you—yes.'

Gabby rolled her eyes. 'So, what *did* Mr Parker say about me?'

'It's always about you, isn't it…?' Paul teased. 'Actually, the guy had an idea that you must have friends in high places. I put him straight. Mind you, I did start to wonder when they sent that car to pick me up. You should have seen it—about twenty feet long, and inside…' He let out a long whistle and shook his head. 'Then I realised.'

'You did?'

He nodded. 'They're buttering me up.'

'They are?'

'Obviously.'

Gabby shook her head and looked bemused.

'God, Gabby, you are so slow sometimes. They're afraid of bad publicity. And— Is that chocolate?' Distracted, he picked up a bar of chocolate that was amongst the contents that had spilled out of Gabby's bag onto the table.

He mimed a roll of drums and said dramatically, 'My first food as a free and exonerated man.' He shoved a large chunk into his mouth, rolled his eyes and groaned. 'Heaven,' he said, before adding, 'The thing is, they don't want me suing them for false imprisonment or something.'

Gabby's eyes widened in alarm. 'You're not thinking of doing anything like that, are you, Paul?' she asked uneasily.

'All I want to do is go home.'

Gabby's shoulders sagged in relief. 'You're booked on the six-thirty flight this evening.'

'Six-thirty? That barely gives me time to use room service.' Paul flung himself down on the nearest sofa and threw a grateful look at Gabby. 'You're a miracle-worker, sis.' His expression sobered as he asked, 'How are Mum and Dad?'

'You can ask them yourself later today.'

'It's been tough on them.'

She nodded. 'They've coped well enough.'

'Is there cable? Do you think I could get the match?' Paul wondered.

Gabby, thinking of the anxiety she'd suffered, imagining him in some cell with no window, regarded Paul with amused exasperation. He had just been through an experience that would have traumatised most and permanently scarred some for life, and all he could think of was a soccer match. And it wasn't an act either.

It must be nice, she reflected wistfully, to go through life with such a laid-back attitude.

'Was it terrible? Prison?' Gabby asked, feeling as usual like the responsible adult present, even though Paul was six years older than her.

Paul began to scroll through the channels, stopping when he found a cartoon he proclaimed to be his favourite.

'If you don't want to talk about it, I understand.'

'Turn down the empathy, Gabby, it's not good for your blood pressure. I've not got post-traumatic stress or anything. What is there to say? It's not meant to be nice, is it? It's prison. But it wasn't as bad as it might have been, and I knew I'd get out. I hadn't done anything, and anyhow I had the A team on the job.' He shot her an affectionate grin.

Gabby responded, marvelling at the way he had shrugged off his imprisonment the same way he shrugged off anything unpleasant that ever happened to him. Paul was, she reflected, nothing if not resilient.

'You look different.'

Gabby was amazed that he had noticed. 'You think so?'

'New dress?'

'Yes,' she agreed, thinking, New dress, new hair, new make-up… In fact when she had looked in the mirror before she had driven—or rather *been* driven—out of the palace earlier, she had hardly recognised the person who had looked back at her. If Paul, not the most observant of people, had noticed, the transformation must be even greater than she had thought.

'It's a different look,' Paul observed, fingering the blue filmy fabric of the skirt that fell in soft folds to her knees.

'But you don't like it?'

'Sure. I'm just used to seeing you in jeans. This makes you look a bit…um…untouchable,' he decided, studying her new look.

'Untouchable?'

Gabby was startled by the suggestion, but when she thought about it was not exactly displeased. The chances of Prince Hakim wanting to touch her were in her opinion fairly remote, and if she was cold and distant enough it would hopefully put him off her totally. Throwing many obstacles in the way of Rafiq's plan could only be a good thing. And if, as she suspected, Rafiq was overestimating his brother's sense of duty, it would not be long before Rafiq had to accept that people were not puppets.

But it was not her ability to be cold and distant to his brother that was troubling Gabby. Every time she thought of the way she had grabbed Rafiq and kissed him she wanted to curl up and die—and when she thought of him kissing her back the recognition that she hadn't wanted him to stop was more than humiliating, it was beyond belief!

How was it possible? The feelings he had aroused in her were terrifying, the hunger and excitement totally alien to her nature. Why, of all the men she had ever met, was this angry, tragic, *infuriating* man the one who had awoken the dormant sensual side to her nature?

Of course he had a good side. She kept seeing his tired, beautiful face as Sayed had arrived at the Bahu encampment to escort her back to the palace yesterday. He cared so passionately about his people and his country that she couldn't help but admire him and worry about him.

She clenched her teeth. No, she *wouldn't* worry! The wretched man hadn't even had the courtesy to let her know when or if he had returned to the palace. All she'd had was that stupid damned note this morning!

What was wrong with her? Was she one of those women who were attracted to what they couldn't have?

No. For that theory to work she would have to *want* Prince Rafiq, and obviously she didn't. Heat ignited low in her belly just thinking of him, but that was only a chemical reaction to a man who was the quintessence of everything male. Small wonder, really, that her hormones had been jolted out of their dormant state.

But she had them firmly under control now, so it was end of story, turn the darned page, Gabby, and get on with sorting out the next problem—namely, showing she was not queen material.

'Well, maybe not untouchable, but…' Paul replied.

'Regal?' Gabby suggested. Gabby, appalled by her thought, struggled with the urge to mess her hair and wipe off the beautifully applied make-up. All day she'd had the feeling of being trapped inside the body of someone else. Or maybe just trapped—which she was. *Temporarily* trapped.

Paul threw back his head and laughed. 'You? Regal? Now, that *is* a good one.' He chuckled at the joke, then asked, 'What time did you say the flight was?'

Gabby told him and he consulted his watch. 'So, no time for a nap?'

She shook her head. 'I don't suppose it was easy to sleep in prison?'

'Actually, there wasn't a lot else to do—and you know me. I can sleep anywhere, any time. The King of the Catnap!' he said, stretching out on the sofa and yawning. 'Haven't you got some packing to do or something? Shall I order a taxi?'

Gabby took a deep breath. 'Actually, Paul, I thought I might stay on for a while.'

'You're not coming home?'

Home. The emotional lump of loss in Gabby's throat swelled, and she blinked as she felt the prickle of tears behind her eyelids.

She could get on that plane with Paul.

She had given her word, but that had been under duress so it didn't count. There was nothing barring the integrity Rafiq seemed so convinced she possessed stopping her. She could sleep in her own bed tonight.

The idea held a lot of appeal.

What was to stop her? *Who* was to stop her?

Rafiq? Even Rafiq would stop short of boarding an international flight and hauling her off—wouldn't he? An image of Rafiq's face—the carved cheekbones, the sensually sculpted mouth and the implacable dark eyes—flashed into her mind.

It was the face of a man who would stop short of nothing to achieve the goal he had set himself. The man was so fixated and stubborn that she was wasting her time telling him his plan was crazy, but she was sure that the passage of time would prove what he didn't want to hear.

'I thought I'd take an extended holiday,' she said.

Just the odd twenty years or so, if things went according to Rafiq's plan. But it wouldn't—it *couldn't*. Gabby clung to her conviction. The alternative was something she couldn't bring herself to contemplate.

'But you don't *go* on holiday.'

'I don't go on holiday as often as you—but then who does?'

Paul worked only to pay for his trips, while their parents lived in hope that he would outgrow his wanderlust, but so far it showed no signs of happening.

'I went to the Lake District last summer,' she reminded him.

Paul dismissed the Lake District with a grimace. 'You took a group of kids and you camped in the rain. I don't call that a holiday.'

'The Lake District is beautiful.'

Paul shook his head. 'You know, Gabby, sometimes I worry about you. Maybe I'll stay on with you.'

The word exploded from Gabby. *'No!'*

She felt Paul's astonished stare, and added in a more moderate tone, 'What I mean is, you have to go home. This has been traumatic for Mum and Dad, and they're not going to believe you're safe until they see you and hug you.'

Paul grimaced and looked contrite. 'Point taken. Poor Mum and Dad—I've given them a tough time over the years, haven't I? I never mean for these thing to happen, you know.'

Gabby's expression softened with affection. 'I know you don't.'

'Well, at least they have one kid who doesn't give them nightmares.'

Gabby dodged his gaze. She was still working on the assumption that Rafiq's plan would never actually come to fruition, but if it did it would not be just her own life that was affected.

She tuned back in from her worried analysis just in time to hear Paul say, 'Shame, though. I'd have liked to show you the sights… Not jail, obviously. Are you staying on at this hotel? How much are they asking a night? Let me speak to the management—I'll see if they'll do you a deal.'

'Thanks, Paul, but actually I've had an invite to stay with…a family.'

'Cool—the best way to see a country is to stay with locals. Or are they ex-pats?'

'No, they're local, actually. I've been invited to stay at the palace.'

Paul stared at her. After a long, startled silence he clapped his hands and gave a smug smile. 'See—I was right!'

'You were?' she said warily.

'Yeah. They're scared stiff I'll stir up trouble and they're pulling a charm offensive on you. I say go for it, sis. You might even get to see the Royals.'

'I can hardly wait.'

'I was just joking. That place is vast—and you're not likely to get invited to dinner with the King.'

Gabby, her mind very much on the ordeal awaiting her that evening, joined in weakly as Paul laughed heartily at his own joke.

'Come on,' she said, playfully knocking his foot down from the sofa. 'Shake a leg. You don't want to miss your flight.'

* * *

'What did I tell you?' Paul said as she climbed into the limo beside him. 'VIP treatment. I'm tempted to stay and milk it a bit.'

'They might be tempted to change their mind and throw you back into jail.'

Paul laughed and patted her hand. 'You're such a worrier, Gabby.'

At the airport the VIP treatment continued. They were even shown through to a private lounge and offered refreshments. Gabby had a few moments' panic when the flight was called and Paul was nowhere to be found, but he returned before she had gone into meltdown, looking pleased with himself.

'Where were you? The flight has been called.'

'First class,' he announced as she hustled him out of the lounge. 'Now do you believe me?'

She smiled and shook her head. 'You're incorrigible. But promise me one thing—don't talk to any strange women.'

'I've sworn off women.'

'I've heard that before,' Gabby muttered as she watched him go through security.

The relief she felt as she watched Paul's flight lift off was intense.

He was safe. She had achieved what she came out here to do. But at a price.

The heat outside the air-conditioned terminal building hit Gabby like a solid shimmering wall as she stepped onto the wide pavement in front.

There was no sign of the car that had deposited them, and Gabby was wondering what to do next when a long black limo with tinted windows pulled up.

The rear door opened.

'Get in,' a disembodied voice snapped.

It was the verbal equivalent of a click of the fingers. Gabby's lips thinned in displeasure. She would have given a lot not to jump in in response, but she had very little option.

'Is that an invitation or an order?'

'It's whichever works.'

With a snort, Gabby slid into the back seat. She arranged her skirts neatly around her knees and crossed her ankles, but she was only delaying the inevitable. She had to look at him some time.

'How did you find your brother? He is well?'

As if he actually cared. With anger in her eyes, Gabby turned her head and promptly forgot what she had been about to say.

Today, along with a traditional flowing white robe, his head was covered by a white *keffiyah*, held in place by a woven gold band. The only blemish on his face was the healing wound on his forehead. The traditional headgear emphasised the remarkable bones, the sybaritic purity and the strongly sensual quality of his face. Especially, she thought, the sensual quality of his mouth. Her eyes were irresistibly drawn to the blatantly sexual curve of his lips. It was obvious that a man with a mouth like that had to be a good kisser—and he was.

It was some time later that her drifting, dreamy gaze finally connected with his. He arched a questioning brow. Embarrassed colour flew to her pale cheeks.

She compressed her lips and tossed him a cold response. 'Considering what he's been through, he's remarkably well.' She sniffed and thought, *No thanks to you!*

'You have explained the situation?'

'You mean did I tell him I bought his freedom by relinquishing mine? Strangely enough, no, I didn't. This may seem like some sort of business deal to you, but to most people it would look like blackmail—and, actually, that's how it feels.'

And you're telling him this why? Rafiq is not interested in how you feel.

Instead of answering her outburst with some cutting riposte or sinister warning he didn't say anything at all. But she could feel his eyes, even though she had turned her head and was staring blindly out of the window. Finally she could bear it no longer. She turned her head.

Rafiq was scowling at her.

She lifted her hands like someone protesting their innocence. 'What? It's the truth. Can you say you *haven't* blackmailed me?'

'What have you done to yourself?'

The seemingly unconnected criticism made her blink. 'Done to myself? I haven't done anything.'

He lifted a hand and inscribed a motion above his own head. 'Your hair…your face.'

'That wasn't me—that was your hit squad. You don't like it?' She just managed to stop herself touching her hair.

'I do not like it.'

'How very rude of you to mention it.' And how totally ridiculous that I actually care.

'Why did you let them do this to you?'

The utter unfairness took her breath away. 'Like me, they were following orders—*yours*!'

Her orders had been delivered on a silver tray. Along with details of her brother's flight and where she could meet him, the handwritten note had also informed her that she would be dining that evening with the two Princes. The postscript had explained that a selection of suitable outfits would be delivered to her room later.

They had been—along with a hairdresser, a stylist and a make-up artist. They had admired her skin until Gabby had let slip that her skincare regime was a bit hit and miss, and depended greatly on what skincare products were on special offer. The women had then discovered a lot more room for improvement.

Rafiq looked outraged. 'I did not tell them to do *this!*'

'*This?*' This time she couldn't stop herself touching her hair. 'What's wrong with it? I've been styled, made over…' And apparently I still don't make the grade—great!

'You could be any woman in the street.'

Only the ones who could afford couture, she thought. 'No—any woman in the street could catch a plane and go back home.'

'Your style is individual.' His frowning scrutiny returned to her hair, which shone like glass and fell river-straight down her back.

'That's what I thought you wanted to get rid of.'

Rafiq did not respond. His expression, as he continued to stare at her hair, was distracted. Then without warning he reached out and swept a strand of shiny hair from her cheek.

'That's what I thought too.' But he had changed his mind.

Gabby stared at the blood-red stone on his finger and shivered as his fingertips brushed her cheek.

'Yesterday your hair looked as if you hadn't combed it. When you were sleeping, you…' He speared his fingers deeper into it, and remembered doing the same when he had kissed her. The memory made it hard to retain his detachment. It made him hard, full-stop.

Gabby hardly recognised the hoarse, husky

voice as her own as she retorted, 'I don't always look that bad. Yesterday I had been sleeping in the desert.'

'And worrying about me.' His hand dropped and his hooded stare darkened as his long fingers curled around her throat.

Gabby felt the light touch like a burning brand on her skin. 'I was worried about everyone. How are…?'

The relief she felt when his hand fell away was so intense she had to bite back a bubble of hysterical laughter.

'Two are still on the critical list.'

'I'm sorry.' She was utterly bewildered, and had no way of articulating her helpless physical response to this man. She had never experienced anything like the sensations that were thrumming through her body. So much for taking control of her hormones!

She ran her tongue along her upper lip to blot the beads of moisture that had broken out there, fighting the desire to crawl out of her skin.

'Well, I suppose it's too late to do anything about your hair now.'

'You really know how to make a girl feel good about herself. You could always chuck me out of the car to try and get the look you apparently liked so much,' she said, reaching for the door handle.

With a curse he leaned across her and clamped his hand over hers.

Gabby shrank back in her seat, her senses spinning and her pulses leaping as his arm pressed her into the seat.

'I was joking,' she said. But not now. Now jumping seemed a pretty safe alternative to having him this close. She was overwhelmingly conscious at a cellular level of his hard male body, the heat, the scent, the raw, powerful masculinity of him.

His hand still covering hers, he turned his head. His face was so close she could feel his breath on her cheek and see the network of fine lines around his eyes. His dark hooded eyes were fierce and hypnotic.

And then it came. The forbidden thought she had walled away—*he's dying*.

A keening cry ached for escape from her tight throat. She shouldn't feel this terrible sense of loss—for God's sake, she didn't even like him, he was her enemy—but the empathic connection she felt with him was so strong she could feel the weight of his emotional isolation, and her foolish heart ached for him.

How do I feel so close to this man?

Their eyes connected and clung, and for a moment time seemed to slow, then freeze. It was Rafiq who leaned back in his seat, and the spell broke.

Gabby expelled a shaky sigh and sat on her hands, to hide the fact they were shaking. 'Talk

about overreaction. You have no sense of humour.'
She gave a light laugh and turned her head to look
out of the window. Please let this journey be over!

The highway from the airport was wide, long
and straight, cutting directly through miles of flat
ochre-coloured desert, dotted with strange and
weirdly shaped rock formations that rose up into the
sky, casting even weirder shadows against the desert
floor. There was a lot of traffic. She commented on
the fact, because it seemed like a fairly safe and impersonal subject.

'It is a holiday here and it is tradition for
people—families—to go to the sea. They are now
returning to the city.'

'I know someone who took a diving holiday
here a few a years ago.'

'Yes, there is good diving. The coast is littered with
wrecks that are rich in sea life. I learnt to dive there
myself.'

'And those green patches I keep seeing in the
desert? What are they?' she asked, looking at his
cut glass profile and not at the scenery rushing by.

'They are areas of irrigation, and most productive. We actually have a strong agricultural
economy, and even without the hand of man the
desert is not as arid and lifeless as it appears. Many
species have adapted to the conditions and temper-
ature fluctuations—I have even seen fig trees
growing miles from water.'

Gabby listened, fascinated as much by the passion, enthusiasm and pride for his country she could hear in his voice as the information.

'In the south, where there is no shortage of rainfall, we have—' He stopped abruptly and turned his head. 'Are you actually interested?'

Gabby said the first thing that came into her head. Unfortunately it was the truth.

'No, I just like the sound of your voice.' Actually, *like* was far too tepid a term. 'And of course,' she continued, adopting a flippant attitude, 'I'm going to be Queen of all I survey…' *Quick recovery, Gabby.* Her mocking smile faded. 'You do know it's not going to happen, don't you, Rafiq?' she said quietly. 'Have you even told your family that you're ill?'

'I will tell them at the appropriate time,' he replied with deceptive calm. The problem was one that he knew he would have to face. But not yet.

His father was not young, and though he was not a physically demonstrative man Rafiq knew that his sons were his life. Once people knew he would be treated differently, and this was something he wanted to postpone for as long as possible.

'They have a right to know,' Gabby began earnestly. 'And you shouldn't be alone. You should have—'

Rafiq listened until he could bear no more. 'Enough!' He cut her dead with a jerky motion of his hand. 'I hardly need a support network when I have you, do I?'

His sarcasm made her flush and look away—but not before Rafiq had seen the glitter of tears in her eyes.

He studied her delicate profile and felt glad there was no woman in his life who would weep tears for him and mourn. What man could contemplate the prospect of the woman he had held in his arms and made love to watching him fade away by slow degrees without horror?

'Let me make it plain that I do not need your pity, your understanding, or your compassion. Is that clear?'

She swallowed and compressed her lips. 'As crystal.'

His voice soft with menace, he leaned in towards her, his dark eyes burning into hers. 'And if you have any ideas about telling anyone…'

'I won't blab.'

'Good,' he said, settling back in his seat as the car glided through the open palace gates.

CHAPTER TEN

'WE ARE dining in the small family dining room.'

'Cosy. *Very* cosy,' she commented as he stood aside to let her precede him into the room. The 'small family dining room' was the size of a football pitch. The table set at one end, with gold candlesticks, heavy crystal and antique silver, was about thirty feet long, and they were walking on a mosaic floor that had to be centuries old.

Rafiq, upon whom her irony was wasted, saw her staring at the glowing mosaic and said casually, 'Byzantine,' before approaching the man sitting at the table with a newspaper propped in front of him.

Gabby looked curiously at the man she was meant to marry. *It just so was not going to happen.* He was around six feet tall and slim, and he wore his dark hair cropped short and spiky at the front. A black tee shirt under a silver-grey suit and scuffed trainers completed his ensemble.

The same individuality and lack of formality

was evident in his greeting, as he clapped his elder brother on the back and regarded Gabby with open curiosity.

'Hello, I'm Hakim. You must be Gabriella. I've heard a lot about you.'

Gabby's eyes widened. 'You have?' She threw Rafiq a questioning glare before accepting the hand extended to her. Her fixed smile broadened when the young Prince held her eyes and raised it to his lips.

Gabby laughed, and realised that staying distant and cold was not going to be easy. 'Sorry—you just remind me of someone I know.'

His smile flashed white in his handsome face. 'Someone pretty marvelous—am I right?'

Gabby laughed again. 'My brother—and he would be the first to agree with you.' Her glance flickered between the two Princes. Rafiq scowled and Hakim winked. 'Gosh, you're not even a little bit alike, are you?' she gasped, thinking that the younger brother might be all style over substance, but he was charming and refreshingly uncomplicated to someone struggling to cope with the exhausting complexity, contradictions and convolutions of Rafiq's personality.

'You see, Rafiq, some people appreciate me.'

The duration of the meal followed the same pattern of light-hearted banter—though there was a slight hiccough when, in the middle of dessert, Hakim asked her how the research for her thesis was going.

Gabby played for time. *'Thesis?'*

'Gabriella has not yet had an opportunity to see first-hand the new initiative for the Bedouin children,' Rafiq inserted, in response to her raised eyebrow glare.

'Well, you're in safe hands with Rafiq, Gabriella.'

Safe was not exactly the word that sprang to mind when she thought of Rafiq's hands. She swallowed, thinking of them framing her face while he kissed her. Her eyes were drawn unwisely to the sensuous, sexy curve of his lips. Rafiq saw her looking and his eyes went hot when he felt her gaze. Her stomach went into a dipping dive.

'Gabby,' she said at last, her voice a little too breathy and her smile several thousand volts too bright. To her relief Hakim seemed oblivious to the charged undercurrents that she could feel like a crackle under her skin.

'Gabby—I like that. Well, Gabby, the entire idea was Rafiq's brainchild. As you can imagine, there was a lot of local opposition to combat—especially when he insisted that females have full access to the scheme. So, you're in education Gabby?'

'I'm an infant school teacher.'

'Really? You look nothing like any teacher had. Does she, Rashid?'

His appeal to his brother was met with a blank stare. Just when the silence was getting awkward, Rafiq responded, 'Gabriella is very well qualified.'

'I'm sure she is. What I'm wondering is how you two met.'

'By accident.'

'A mutual friend.'

The two versions emerged simultaneously.

Gabby glared at Rafiq, who carried on eating—or actually not. She had already noted with some concern that all he did was push his food around the plate—a fact which seemed to have escaped the notice of his brother.

Hakim looked amused as he glanced from one to the other. 'Obviously it was a fate thing.'

Gabby's embarrassment increased when several more comments Hakim made through the meal revealed—to her at least—that he was obviously under the impression that she and Rafiq were an item.

Rafiq, whose contribution to social intercourse had shrunk to monosyllabic grunts by the end of the meal, seemed oblivious. And the gaps in conversation were ably filled by Hakim, who was happy to talk—especially about himself.

Having toyed with her dessert, and getting increasingly angry because she was concerned about Rafiq, Gabby excused herself and retired to her room. The man might be in terrible agony, and he was too stupid or stubborn to say a word. He'd just sat there looking noble and dignified because he didn't know how to act any other way.

After pacing the room making unflattering observations about the Crown Prince of Zantara, while fractured images and snatches of conversation played in her head, it hit her like the proverbial bolt from the blue.

She—the woman with the armour-plated heart—had fallen in love. With the wrong brother! How funny was that?

She didn't feel much like laughing as, hand pressed to her forehead, she fell full-length backwards onto the bed and lay there, staring blankly up at the ceiling.

She had fallen in love with a man who, even if he'd had a future, would have had no place for her in it. Did irony get any darker? Did life get any more darned unfair? Tears began to seep from beneath her eyelids, streaming unchecked down her face.

Rafiq nodded to the maid who had brought coffee and turned to his brother. 'You appeared to get on well with Miss Barton, Hakim? What did you think of her?'

He had to work hard to keep the note of accusation from his voice, and he was not entirely successful. It seemed an appropriate moment to remind himself that this was what he wanted, what he had actively engineered—more than he had in all honesty expected.

He had expected Gabriella to make herself as obnoxious as she knew how—and he knew from personal experience that was *very*. Instead she had laughed at his brother's jokes—even when they weren't funny. That damned dimple of hers had not taken a rest.

There had been an instant rapport between the two. His thoughts slipped back to a moment midway through the meal when he had seen their heads close together, fair and dark almost touching. Hakim had placed his hand on her shoulder and Rafiq had felt a savage compulsion to drag his brother from his seat.

Rafiq inhaled and closed his eyes, his nostrils flaring, the muscles along his angular jaw flexing and tensing, causing the sinews in his neck to stand out like steel cords.

He had been acting like an old wolf—the pack leader about to be replaced by young blood.

It was pathetic.

Why should he be jealous of his brother?

The answer was shocking in its simplicity: because Hakim would have Gabriella. She was everything that didn't attract Rafiq in a woman, and yet he wanted her more than any woman he had ever met. He could not look at her without thinking about touching her skin, inhaling her scent…

'Think of her?' Hakim looked startled by the question. 'It's not like you to ask my opinion.'

'Well, I'm asking now.'

'I haven't really thought…' Rafiq's dark accusing frown made Hakim backtrack. 'She's nice, very pretty—a bit *serious*…'

Rafiq's face went blank with utter astonishment. Were they talking about the same woman? 'Serious…? You mean *not* shallow? And this is a bad thing?'

'I didn't mean it that way. I meant…studious-serious,' Hakim corrected, thinking his brother must *really* like this English teacher to spring to her defence that way.

Not really news. A man would have had to be blind and deaf not to have noticed the obvious charge crackling between them. And in his experience only people who were *very* aware of one another ignored one another quite so determinedly.

It was not amazing that Rafiq was attracted to Gabby—she was pretty gorgeous—but it was amazing…actually, more than amazing…that Rafiq was discussing her with him. He had always kept his personal life strictly private, and there had been no male bonding sessions when they were younger, where they exchanged stories about the women who had broken their hearts.

Hakim's heart had frequently been broken, but if Rafiq had ever lost a night's sleep over a woman it was news to him.

'*Studious?*' Rafiq echoed, thinking of her soft, naked and pliant in his arms...while she was asleep at least. Awake, she had turned into a spitting little wild cat.

'All right, then, smart, clever. I find that a bit...intimidating.' He shrugged and grinned. 'Because, unlike you, brother, I'm not what you'd call intellectual, I generally go for girls who are more—'

Rafiq, looking pained, cut across his brother. 'Details are unnecessary. I have seen the sort of girls you *like*.'

Hakim grinned broadly. 'I'm what you'd could call a work in progress. But one of these days, brother, I might just surprise you.' *And sooner than you think*, he added silently. 'And I do like Gabby. What is not to like...? I presume that you're about to tell me?'

Rafiq lifted a brow. 'Is that what you think?'

'You usually warn me off unsuitable women. I'm amazed you introduced her to me—went out of your way to introduce her to me if she's got a skeleton in the closet. And since when were you interested in what *I* think?'

A spasm of regret crossed Rafiq's dark features. 'I am sorry if I have excluded you, Hakim,' he said abruptly.

Hakim stared. 'Well, if that sorrow is worth a new Porsche—great. I'm really not all that scarred because I haven't sat in on endless meetings on agricultural policy.' His eyes narrowed, and despite the levity of his manner there was some concern in his face as he asked, 'What is all this hair-shirt stuff, Rafiq?'

His eyes widened again as a fairly revolutionary possibility hit him. Was it possible Rafiq was asking his *advice*? Or at least asking for him to tell him to go for it, even if she didn't tick all the boxes?

He must *really* like her!

'What do you need my opinion for anyway? Are you trying to tell me that you haven't already got a file an inch thick on Gabby?' Hakim knew that his brother entered into relationships the same way he would a financial negotiation. He did his research and was not flexible. He did not make concessions.

But this time it looked as if whatever dirt he had on the girl in question had not put him off. But perhaps he thought it should? Who knew? Hakim thought. They were in new territory.

The file Hakim had spoken of had indeed arrived in its more complete form, on his desk that morning. Rafiq had put it straight in a locked drawer, telling himself that he would study it later.

But no matter what was in that file, no matter what or who lay in Gabriella's past, it would not alter the fact that she'd make a better wife than his brother deserved, and would be a queen that any country would be proud to boast of.

'What a woman did before she met you is hardly important.'

Hakim, in the act of stirring more sugar into his coffee, stopped and turned to stare at his brother in utter amazement. Rafiq was serious... How serious...? *Wife* serious?

'So if you decided to get married tomorrow you wouldn't want to know ahead of time if your prospective bride had any scandals that might be embarrassing?'

'The same premise applies.'

Hakim's jaw dropped. 'Is this the same man speaking who once told me that a royal bride needs to be squeaky clean, no unsavoury secrets, no skeletons in the closet. The next thing you'll be telling me is she doesn't have to be a virgin.'

Rafiq did not join in his brother's amused laughter. 'It is better to be the last man in a woman's life than the first.' Better, of course, to be both. But Rafiq appreciated that in the modern world that limited a man's choices. *His* choices were non-existent, but Hakim had a life of choices ahead of him. Of course he didn't know how lucky he was, because it was the human way not to appreciate what you had until it was being taken from you.

Hakim stopped laughing and stared. 'Will

whatever alien that has taken over your body let me speak to my brother, Rafiq?'

'Do not be foolish,' Rafiq snapped, his brows knitting into an irritated frown.

'You know what you're talking like?' Hakim fixed his brother with a narrowed, speculative stare. 'You're talking like a man who's fallen in love. Have you ever been in love, Rafiq?'

'Not as often as you, little brother.'

'Clever,' Hakim admired. 'But you didn't answer the question.'

'And I am not going to.'

CHAPTER ELEVEN

'GABBY—Gabby wherefore art thou…?'

Gabby, who had been sitting in a chair staring out over the palace illuminated against a deep velvet starry sky, got to her feet and, standing well back from the edge, looked down cautiously. Prince Hakim was standing beneath the balcony, his hand pressed to his heart and a grin on his handsome face.

'At school,' he called up, 'I always wanted to be Romeo, but being the prettiest boy in school, and until I was seventeen one of the shortest, I was always Juliet.'

'From what I hear you've had a lot of practice playing Romeo since.'

He grimaced. 'Ouch! Someone has been telling tales. If you leaned down I could climb up your hair.'

Gabby lifted a hand to her hair. After a shower it had reverted to type and gone its own sweet way. 'Make up your mind. Am I Juliet or Rapunzel?' she said, throwing a rope of silky blonde threads over her shoulder.

'I wish I could stay around and discover, but alas I'm flying back to Paris tonight.'

'Isn't that a bit unexpected?'

'As a matter of fact, yes. But something my brother said has made my mind up about something…'

'Something Rafiq said…?' Gabby's face fell. 'So he's told you…' She felt relief, and then almost immediately alarm and indignation. 'But you must realise that you can't go!'

'Why can't I go?'

Her words were jumbled in her anxiety to convince him that his dying brother needed him here. 'Oh, I know the stuff about me is a bit crazy, but don't worry—that will blow over. I think it's his way of coping, staying in control. He needs you here. I know he pushes people away, and acts as though he's invincible, but—'

Hakim's voice minus the mockery and laughter sounded much more like his brother's as he cut across her. 'Why does Rafiq need me here?'

'Why?' She closed her eyes and pressed her hand to her mouth—*a bit late now, Barton*. She groaned. 'You don't know, do you?' Oh, God, what had she done?

'Don't know what?'

'I can't tell you. I gave my word.'

Hakim swore at length and then, after first

testing the strength of the wrought-iron support of the balcony, began to climb up it.

From above Gabby watched, her heart in her mouth.

Across the courtyard Rafiq, standing next to an ornate fountain, watched with very different feelings. He had arrived in time to watch the entire scene. Thanks to the noise from the fountain he hadn't been able to hear what was being said, but he had a pretty good idea. He couldn't see them now that Hakim had grabbed her and pushed into the bedroom, but he had a pretty good idea what was happening.

It wasn't going to happen. He wouldn't allow it!

The primal rage that surfaced in him lasted the time it took him to charge across the courtyard and reach the balcony. He stood in the exact spot his brother had. He could see the imprint of his footprints in the freshly watered grass. The rage turned to cold stone inside him.

What was he going to do? Climb up and claim her? Well, that made sense   he had so much more to offer a woman than Hakim. *Take me, because I'm a dying man.*

Half an hour later, when the sprinkler system switched on again, Rafiq was still standing in the same spot. The jets of water roused him from the dark place he had gone to. He let his head fall back and lifted his eyes to the sky as water streamed down his face, and he felt the pain of the primal scream locked in his throat.

He ached for a woman he had pushed into the arms of his brother. He couldn't even summon a smile to recognise the dark irony.

'I'm so, *so* sorry,' Gabby said, falling to her knees beside Prince Hakim, who sat hunched in a chair his face hidden in his hands. 'I thought he had told you.'

Hakim lifted his head. His face was chalk-white and his dark eyes stricken. 'I don't believe it. Rafiq is…he's never been ill a day in his life. Why the hell didn't he tell me?' He turned a resentful glare on Gabby. 'He told *you*.'

'That's because I'm a stranger.'

'I'm his brother.'

'That's the point,' Gabby cried, her tender heart aching. She wasn't hurt by Hakim's hostility, she was just grateful that he hadn't got as far as wondering why she had agreed to Rafiq's scheme.

She laid her hand flat on her chest and said in as neutral a voice as possible, '*I* don't matter to him.' *Why should you, you idiot woman?* 'He wants to protect you for as long as he can,' she explained.

Hakim dragged a hand across his face, blotting the moisture from his red-rimmed eyes. 'He's been protecting me for twenty-four years,' he choked.

'I know,' Gabby said patting his hand. 'The thing is, now we—' She stopped and closed her eyes.

There is no *we*, Gabby. There's *them*. Rafiq and his family. 'You, his family and his friends need to be there for him,' she finished quietly.

'You know, I thought all that stuff at dinner… you and him…I thought *he* wanted to marry you. When all along he thinks I'm so pathetic I can't do the job of king without someone to back me up.' Again his expression was tinged with resentment as he looked at Gabby. 'He must have a very high opinion of you.'

She shook her head. 'No, he thinks I'm a total pain.' She gave a shaky laugh. 'But he loves you,' she told Hakim earnestly. 'And he knows what a desperately hard job you'll have. He's had his whole life to prepare for it, but it's just being dropped on you. He wants to help and he's a control freak.'

Hakim sniffed and smiled. 'He is that. And I'm not offended he thinks I can't cut the mustard. He's right. I can't do it.'

'Do what?'

'Be King.' Hakim got to his feet and dragged a hand through his hair. He walked towards the door, leaving a dismayed Gabby sitting on the floor. 'He's right, Gabby. I can't do it alone. I know I can't.'

It had been almost six a.m. before Gabby had fallen asleep, and it was late when she emerged the next morning. She wasn't surprised to find herself alone eating breakfast.

Or actually not eating. Her stomach rebelled at the thought of food. She wished she knew what was going on. What had Hakim done? Had he gone straight to Rafiq and confronted him? Had he run away? No, she couldn't think that of him—she didn't want to.

Only a week ago she had been reading about this family in an article, a bit of hurried research, and now she had become so deeply embroiled in their lives her own would never be the same.

Damn, if only she'd thought to tell Hakim to wait until Rafiq was ready to tell him the truth. If only she'd kept her mouth shut to begin with and not jumped in with both big feet. She looked down at her size fours, shod in a pair of soft leather sandals, and asked herself, *Why am I blaming myself? I didn't ask to be in the middle of this. I didn't ask to be blackmailed. I didn't ask to fall in love! Damn, damn, damn! What am I going to do?*

Forehead creased against the pounding in her temples, Gabby clapped a hand to her aching head. She felt like a hamster in a wheel, going nowhere fast, her thoughts revolving around in ceaseless unproductive circles.

Bottom line: her life was chaos. She was standing in the middle of an emotional minefield and it didn't make any difference what choice she made, which direction she went—she was going to be hurt.

She didn't want to be a queen. She wanted to be with one man—a brave, stupid man, who was trying to push her into bed with his brother!

Expression stormy, she took a sip from her coffee cup and yelped as the liquid scalded her mouth. She slammed the cup down, splashing coffee all over the snowy table linen, and poured iced water from the pitcher into her glass.

She was greedily gulping it when she saw Sayed in the doorway.

'Miss Barton…'? I am sorry to disturb you.'

Gabby's expression of polite enquiry morphed into one of apprehension when the normally imperturbable Sayed spoke again.

'I am very worried about the Crown Prince, miss.'

She dropped the glass, spilling water over the already ruined table linen.

Her manner was at stark variance to the icy dread that was creeping over her as she smiled politely and asked, 'Has something happened?'

If anything *had* happened she would be the only one, barring Hakim, who realised the ominous implications. Her jaw firmed and her hands balled into tight fists at her sides as she struggled to control her panic. Damn the man for a stubborn idiot.

'I think something must have, miss… He…the Crown Prince…is…angry.'

Gabby expelled a relieved sigh. At least he wasn't ill. 'Is that all? He's always angry.'

Even as she spoke Gabby realised he wasn't—at least not with everyone else. By comparison with his cranky, critical attitude to her, he was capable of displaying an almost supernatural degree of tolerance with other people. Not that he suffered fools gladly, but on the other hand he gave praise where it was due, and people went the extra mile just to receive one of his rare smiles.

Gabby pushed away the image of Rafiq smiling and concentrated on Sayed, who was shaking his head in an emphatic negative motion.

'No, this is serious. I have known the Crown Prince since he was a child, and I have never seen him like this. I am worried,' he confessed.

So was Gabby, though she struggled to hide it. 'Why are you telling me this, Sayed?'

'I thought you might—' He stopped, looking awkward, and began wringing his gnarled hands together.

Gabby took pity on him and suggested, 'You thought I might be stupid enough to risk getting my head chewed off?' Despite her joking tone the genuine anxiety in the older man's eyes filled her with increasing disquiet.

Sayed looked relieved. 'Exactly so, miss. He might listen to you.'

Gabby stared at the man, wondering if he had been out too long in the midday sun. Listen to her? Rafiq did not listen to anyone. But her... She was the very *last* person he would listen to. Somehow the staff here had got the wrong message from her presence.

'So he didn't seem ill at all?'

'Ill, miss?' He shook his head, looking puzzled, adding with a touch of pride, 'No, the Crown Prince enjoys excellent health. He always has, even as a boy.'

Gabby's eyes fell. Even asking if he was ill went against the denial screaming inside her as she refused point-blank to contemplate a world that did not contain Rafiq.

It was bizarre. Not long ago she had not known he even existed, except as a name in the official guidebook. Now the idea of him not being here made bony, skeletal fingers of dread in her chest tighten until she couldn't breathe.

'I'll see what I can do.' She doubted it would be anything of substance, but Sayed obviously thought otherwise: his relief was obvious. The man clearly imagined she possessed supernatural powers. 'Where is he?'

'He is in his private room in the tower, miss. I think you know where it is.'

Gabby saw the man's secret little smile. Clearly the grapevine was alive and well in the Palace. And she for one didn't want to know what garbled version of the truth had been passed around.

* * *

Gabby had lifted her hand to tap on the door when she heard the sound of a loud, angry voice inside. She stopped and waited. There was a short silence after the rant ended, and then the even more alarming sound of crashing and smashing began.

Gabby gave up on the idea of announcing herself. Instead she pushed the door open cautiously. It gave. Wondering what on earth she was going to find, she squared her shoulders and stepped inside.

There was evidence of the destruction she had heard, but there was nothing systematic about it as far as she could see. Rafiq, who was pacing the floor like a sleek, feral caged animal, wasn't simply walking around objects, but through them.

Rafiq turned, a snarl on his face. 'What are *you* doing here?'

Their glances connected, worried blue on wrathful and smouldering black, and her breath snagged painfully in her throat. In his primitive anger all pretence of civilisation was washed away and Rafiq was quite simply magnificent. Of course she had always known he was a man of strong passions, and she had even seen him strain at the emotional leash at times, but now it had snapped!

As their glances connected his eyes, blacker than the darkest starless night sky, lit from within by twin flames, drilled into her. Every individual fibre and muscle in his body was bunched and taut. He was an explosion about to happen.

She didn't want to supply the final trigger. Gabby ran her tongue lightly across her dry lips as something that was part trepidation and part excitement slid through her. Now that really *did* make her weird…

'What has happened, Rafiq? Are you ill? Is—?'

'Not ill—just dying.' He saw her flinch, but pushed away the shaft of inconvenient guilt that slipped like a dull blade between his ribs.

Gabby, her face pale, bit down on her quivering lip and tucked her hair behind her ears. It immediately sprang free. 'Well, something must have happened to put you in this mood.'

His upper lip curled into a sneer. 'Something? Oh, yes, *something* has happened,' he agreed darkly as he swung away from her.

Gabby watched, her frustration growing as he recommenced his restless panther-like pacing of the room. She chased after him, catching him as he reached the doors that lay open to the balcony where she had lost her balance the first time they had met.

Without thinking she caught hold of his arm and tugged him to a stop.

He stood breathing hard, staring with a look she couldn't put a name on at her hand on his arm.

'Sorry—I'm a tactile person.' She sincerely hoped he didn't correctly translate this as *I can't keep my hands off you.* 'I keep forgetting people don't lay hands on the royal person without an invitation.'

She turned her head to one side and regarded him with a calm she was not feeling.

'Will you stop being so damned enigmatic and stay still for ten seconds? You can be snide and superior just as well when you're sitting down. I know this,' she said, placing her hands flat on her chest, 'because I've seen you do it.'

The fury still pounded inside his skull like a hammer, but Rafiq managed a flicker of a smile as he lowered himself into a chair.

'Thank you,' she said, dropping to her knees beside it. 'Now, you can tell me that it's none of my business,' she began, thinking he most probably would, 'but—'

'It *is* your business.'

That threw Gabby off balance. 'It is?'

'I received a note form Hakim this morning. He has flown back to Paris.'

Rafiq watched as the colour drained from her face. If his brother had been on the same continent at that moment he would not have been responsible for his actions.

'How could he? How could he leave now? After…?' Gabby, her face as pale as paper apart from two bright spots of angry colour on the apples of her cheeks, stopped and pressed a hand to her lips. How could he do this to Rafiq?

The pain in her horrified whisper penetrated a part of Rafiq's heart that had never previously been exposed.

She lifted swimming blue eyes to Rafiq. 'I really thought he had more—' Her voice broke as she considered Hakim's departure.

'My brother is a fool, and I am sorry for what he has done to you. His actions are those of a—' He used a word in his native tongue that she didn't understand, but his expression was translation enough.

'Done to *me*?' she echoed, confused.

Rafiq swallowed, the muscles in his throat visibly rippling under his brown skin and his eyes glowing as he contemplated the pleasure of throttling his own brother.

'You have suffered at the hands of the Al Kamil family.' He gave a grimace of self-recrimination. 'I have used you,' he admitted stiffly, his rage visibly growing as he spoke, 'but at least I haven't slept with you, knowing all along I had no intention—' He closed his eyes and cursed slowly and fluently in several languages.

Gabby, her eyes widening suddenly in angry comprehension, exclaimed, 'Slept with me! You think I slept with a man I'd only known five seconds?'

Why not just call me a slut and have done with it? she thought, ignoring the sly voice in her head which suggested that *two* seconds would have done it if the man in question had been Rafiq.

A muscle clenched in his lean cheek as he shook his head in a stiff negative motion. 'You will not speak of it.'

He could not allow himself to think of it, to torture himself with images and allow the jealousy to bite like acid into him.

'But I—'

He cut off her protest with a look. 'I saw him climb into your room.'

Her jaw dropped. 'You saw…?' Her eyes narrowed. 'You were watching?'

'I had something I wished to discuss with you.'

Rafiq had been struggling throughout the day to keep his feelings of guilt at bay, but following their dinner he had come to a decision. He would release her from their bargain. The irony was that, having studied her brother's case in further detail, he doubted that the case against Paul Barton would have ever made it to court after the scheduled review.

Of course this irony had paled into insignificance beside his finding his own brother scaling her balcony—minus the rose between his teeth, but in all other ways the perfect romantic lover.

'I had planned to use the door.'

Gabby bit her lip. 'What did you want to discuss with me?'

'It is no longer relevant.' She was puzzling over his sharp retort when he added, 'To think that I pushed you into his arms!'

His snarled recrimination made Gabby flinch. 'I'm not some puppet. You've never made me do anything I didn't want to, Rafiq.'

Her clumsy attempt to soothe him had the opposite effect.

'So you have fallen in love with him?' he said heavily. It was nothing he had not already suspected. He had seen women fall for his brother's brand of charm before.

The absurd assumption made Gabby stare at this normally smart man. 'Of course not. It was just—'

'Sex?' he finished for her heavily, before closing his eyes and slipping seamlessly into a flood of Arabic she could not follow apart from some spectacular epithets. She watched him slam his fist into the carved arm of his chair.

A cry of alarm was wrenched from the watching Gabby's throat as she witnessed this loss of control.

'For goodness' sake, Rafiq,' she cried, tugging at his arm.

She saw with horror blood well along the line of his knuckles as he ground his flesh into the hard surface. It had to be hurting, but he didn't appear to notice—not the pain, nor her breathless panting efforts to pull his arm down. She could barely get a purchase. The muscles under her fingers were tense and bulging and they had about as much give as a steel bar. Her efforts were futile. He appeared not to even notice her.

He relaxed his arm suddenly, and, breathing a sigh of relief, Gabby knelt there, panting, her fingers still curled around his forearm.

'Your poor hand.' She winced, raising his hand to examine the broken skin across his knuckles. 'You need—'

Rafiq sucked in a deep, shuddering breath and fixed her with a blazing stare so intense it stripped bare her defences, leaving her feeling emotionally exposed and trembling. 'Need…?' he echoed, giving a laugh that made her heart twist in her chest in empathy.

Anger rose inside her as she lifted his hand to her chest and nursed it there. Tears filled her eyes. He needed life, and it was being denied him. Misery lodged in her chest like a lump of lead— there was simply nothing she could say that wasn't utterly clichéd.

'Sorry.'

Her whispered comment brought his eyes to her face. He felt tenderness twist his heart. No woman had ever touched him this deeply.

'I am sorry too. Sorry that I did not imagine for a heartbeat…not for a heartbeat—' He broke off, lifting the hand that she held to his own chest and pressing it against the area where his heart rested.

Gabby, her hand trapped beneath his, could feel the heat of his body and the steady thud of his heart.

Oh, God, but I love him! The anguished admission was drawn from her very soul.

'I did not imagine that a brother of mine could be so totally without honour. He actually left me a note,' he raged, lifting his other hand to frame her face with long brown fingers.

It struck Gabby that to the casual observer they would look like lovers. A shiver slid down her spine.

'What did Hakim say in the letter?' she asked, wondering if she ought to tell Rafiq *why* his brother had gone. It weighed heavily on her conscience that she had inadvertently broken her promise.

But, while unburdening herself might ease her guilt, it was not going to make Rafiq feel any better to know why his brother had run away.

Gabby felt livid every time she thought about the young Prince and his feeble behaviour. She was definitely not inclined to make excuses for him, especially as it seemed to her people had been making excuses for Hakim for too long.

She believed that everyone faced tests in their lives. This was the most important test Hakim had ever faced and he had flunked it! If she had Hakim here now she'd tell him exactly what she thought of him. Of course it hurt like hell to know someone you loved was in pain and that there wasn't a damn thing you could do to help, but you had to put your own feelings to one side.

That was simply what you did when you loved someone. Time enough later to indulge your own pain—too much time, she thought bleakly.

In that moment she was conscious of nothing but Rafiq. Every other thought was obliterated from her head as she soaked in sensations: the warmth radiating from his lean, hard body, his masculine strength, the fresh male scent of his skin.

'People use love as an excuse—as if that justifies everything.'

Gabby felt a moment of guilty panic—*had he guessed?*

Then he added with a sardonic sneer, 'My brother is apparently in love.' Rafiq's fingers fell away from her face, and his upper lip curled with contempt as he contended, 'He doesn't know the meaning of the word.'

Rafiq's eyes swept her face before he turned his head away from her, expelling a hissing breath through flared nostrils. 'He writes to say he is getting married to some woman—a divorcee. Apparently I have said something which has made him realise he has to do this. He never has been able to take responsibility for his own actions.' He flung up his hands in a gesture of disgust before giving a shrug and pronouncing, 'Their children will be idiots.'

'He's getting married?' Gabby cried, sinking back onto her heels. 'I didn't see that one coming,' she admitted, wondering if there really was a woman, or if Hakim had invented her to explain his absence.

Rafiq looked at her downbent head and felt a rush of emotion he avoided analysing. 'My brother is an idiot…' he said. He could have had Gabby, he thought. He is an imbecile!

'You're angry because all your careful plans have gone up in smoke,' she said.

'You think this is about my plans?' It seemed to Gabby that he looked inexplicably startled by her comment.

'But you have to look on the bright side.'

Rafiq followed her advice and realised he would not have to endure the agony of being forced to see her exchange vows with his brother.

'There *is* a bright side?' He was willing to play along. She was clearly putting a brave face on it, but her pride had to be in tatters.

She frowned at the sardonic interruption. 'He will have a wife, and that's what you wanted. She might be good for him.'

'I no longer care.'

Gabby, who didn't for a second believe him, patted his hand—an action that made him stiffen. She would have pulled her hand away, had he not covered it with his own and kept it there.

'Hakim is never going to be you, Rafiq, no

matter who his wife is.' She paused to let this sink in. 'You have to trust him.'

His fingers tightened over hers. 'You of all people can speak my brother's name and say the word trust in the same breath?'

'This isn't about me. I'm just saying you have to let him make his own mistakes, be his own man. This woman might be exactly the sort of wife he needs.'

Rafiq gave her of a look of utter disdain. 'She is—'

'I know—an idiot.'

Her bored drawl pulled him up short. He frowned. 'That is irrelevant.'

This change of tack made Gabby blink. 'Who runs your country is *irrelevant*? I wish you'd decided that before I handed in my notice and gave away my cat.'

He flushed under her sardonic glare. 'My brother's actions to you have been—'

Suddenly Gabby was furious—her temper going from stationary to sixty in the blink of an eye. Shaking with the force of her emotions, she stabbed a finger in the direction of his broad chest. 'Don't you *dare* suggest you're this angry because your brother used me. You're such a hypocrite, Rafiq! This sudden concern for my welfare is totally phoney. This is about the fact that for once you can't control everything!'

'Control?' The irony struck him forcibly. He had never felt as out of control in his life!

'You're a control freak. And you know some-thing? *You're* the idiot!' She stopped and laughed at his stunned expression, barely conscious of the tears running down her cheeks. 'You're so busy preparing for after you're dead—'

She stopped, her voice cracking emotionally as she pulled her hand from his and angrily brushed the moisture from her cheek with the back of her hand.

'You're so busy preparing that you're not both-ering to live the rest of your life. It's an utter waste!' she finished on a resentful quiver. 'You should be extracting every last ounce from—' Shaking her head, she turned away, her teeth drawing blood from her quivering lower lip.

There was silence as Rafiq looked at her slender shoulders shaking.

She started as he laid a hand on her shoulder. 'I'm fine,' she sniffed defensively, before he could say anything. 'I'm not the one dying,' she added thickly.

Oh, God, why had she said that?

CHAPTER TWELVE

RAFIQ, his stern features set like stone, allowed his hand to fall from her shoulder.

'I suppose I'll be going home now?' Gabby said in a small voice.

'Home?'

Gabby turned, tilting her head and looking him directly in the face. She took a deep breath. Had she imagined it? The sizzle of electricity when their hands brushed? The gleam of hunger she had glimpsed in his face when she had felt his eyes on her? Was the entire sexual tension thing a figment of her imagination?

Was it all one-sided?

You'll never know if you don't ask, Gabby. So ask, girl.

'Well, there's no reason for me to stay around here any more—*is* there?'

He met her steady regard with a look that held about as much promise as a wet Monday morning. Gabby felt the metallic taste of humiliation and utter loss in her mouth as she pinned on a smile and gave a jaunty shrug.

'I'll just chalk this up to experience. I got what I came here for—Paul is free—and I've had a nice little holiday thrown in.'

'You are going home?' he said, in the oddest voice.

'Yes, I'm going home!' she yelled in exasperation. 'Haven't I just been saying that for the past—?' She sniffed and blinked back the warm tears welling in her eyes.

The evidence of tears shimmering in her blue eyes drew a curse from his lips. 'You *want* to go home?'

His throaty drawl rasped across her nerve-endings like sandpaper. 'Never mind about what *I* want. For goodness' sake, Rafiq, what about what *you* want?' Her mouth twisted into a bitter smile when he looked at her blankly. 'You act as though I'm talking a foreign language… Well, I suppose I am in a way—not that your English isn't actually better than mine, and—'

His voice cut across her rambling dialogue. 'A man cannot always have what he wants,' he said heavily.

'Just for one minute pretend you can,' she suggested. 'Forget you're a prince, forget duty and family.' She looked at his face, stopped and shook her head. 'There's no point, is there? You can't. You'll always be a prince first and a man second.'

He swallowed. 'Do you think I do not wish it otherwise at times?' he asked harshly.

Her eyes, blue as cornflowers, flew to his face and clung. 'Then wish now,' she begged huskily. 'Forget your brother. You're the one,' she reminded him, 'who always says you don't waste time and effort over things outside your control.'

'I had no idea you had listened to what I say.'

'I hang on your every word,' she drawled sarcastically.

'Your logic is questionable.'

'So is my sanity, when I've been talking to *you* for more than thirty seconds. You know I'm right,' she claimed shakily. 'You just can't admit it. So try to stop being a control freak for two seconds. Forget about your family. I do know this is sacrilege I'm talking…'

'Since when has that stopped you?'

It wasn't the dry insert but the flash of amused warmth that for a brief moment lightened the tension in his features, making Gabby stumble over her words as she continued. 'Forget—f.. forget about Zantara,' she recommended. 'Zantara will be here long after we are *all* gone. Think for once in your life about you.'

'Me?'

'Yes, think about Rafiq,' she said, her blue eye earnestly scanning his face. 'What do you want? And I don't mean duty. I mean what do you *want*? If you could have whatever you want at this minute what would it be? I bet you haven't even thought about it.'

In a world where nothing was the way it should have been this was one thing she was determined to achieve. Rafiq was for once in his life going to do something selfish.

A nerve in his lean cheek jumped as his restless dark glance touched the soft curve of her full mouth. He had gone to sleep seeing her mouth, imagining tasting the sweetness within. He had woken up and the mental torture had continued.

The words were dragged from his throat against his will. 'Oh, I have thought about it.'

'You have? Great!' she enthused, offering him a smile of gentle encouragement. 'So what is it?'

There was a long, dragging silence as his heavy lids came down. Through the mesh of his lashes as they lay against his slashing cheekbones it was impossible for Gabby to read his expression, and he evinced a great interest in his hand-tooled leather riding boots before rising to his feet.

Gabby's soft features hardened into a mask of determination as she followed his example, and stood toe to toe with him. She planted her hands on her softly curved hips and angled her face up to his.

'I'm not moving until you tell me.'

Rafiq's heavy lids lifted. The intensity of his stare burned into Gabby as their eyes met. She was suddenly overwhelmingly conscious of his sheer physical presence as he towered over her. She had no control over the shiver of illicit excitement that trickled down her spine.

'This.'

Gabby's eyes flew wide in startled shock as he bent his dark head towards her. *He's going to kiss me.* The shocking realisation sent a wild rush of heat through her body.

Without thinking—why think about something she had been genetically programmed from birth to do?—she turned her mouth into his, shivering with anticipation at the first firm touch of his lips. A deep sigh shuddered through her body as her lips parted of their own volition under the firm pressure. Her lashes fluttered like trapped butterflies against her flushed cheeks as the kiss deepened and grew more intense, and a fractured lost moan was dragged from somewhere deep inside her.

The heat inside Gabby built as Rafiq continued to kiss her, deepening the intimacy by slow sensual increments as he explored the soft, sweet moistness of her mouth like a starving man who had found sustenance.

She was burning up from the inside out, and the flames of desire were searing away the last threads of common sense from her brain. She knew it was only sex for him, and he thought it was just as casual for her—he believed she had slept with his brother the previous night—but that didn't matter. None of it mattered.

If this was his way of blanking out the cruel cards fate had dealt him, his way of forgetting what must haunt his every waking moment, she didn't care. Gabby wanted to give what comfort she could and take whatever came her way.

Finally Rafiq's head lifted, but he stayed close— close enough for her to be able to feel his warm breath on her face, to see the network of lines radiating from around his eyes.

Gabby looked up at him through half-closed eyes, the hot summer blue almost swallowed up by her dilated pupils. She was trembling, and she could feel the febrile shudders that ran at irregular intervals through his greyhound-lean frame.

She felt a hot, heavy lethargy as he tangled his fingers deep in her hair and ran a finger softly along the curve of her cheek, lingering over the indentation of her dimple.

'I have thought about it a *lot*,' he slurred thickly.

Gabby was intoxicated by the startling admission. 'Then why on earth didn't you do something sooner?' she wailed, standing on her tiptoes to plant a kiss at the corner of his fascinating mouth. He responded with a growl, and kissed her with a ferocity that sent her senses spinning.

'You were marrying my brother,' he reminded

her, when he had kissed her into a state of blissful, aching submission.

Gabby looked up at him. Who would have guessed that surrender to her own needs and those of someone else could feel so perfect?

'And now I'm surplus to requirements?' Bless Hakim, she thought, smiling.

'Not *my* requirements.'

Rafiq turned a deaf ear to the voice in his head that told him he ought not to be doing this. Every fibre in his body told him he *had* to do this—he could no more *not* do this than he could stop his body dragging in its next breath. His brain supplied a plausible cover story that allowed him to go on. This was just sex.

The expression in his eyes made the heat in her blood pool low between her legs. 'Those requirements,' she admitted, with an uncharacteristic boldness she was actually getting the hang of quite quickly, 'are the only ones I'm actually concerned with right now.'

A sudden frown tautened his strong-boned features. 'You are offering yourself up as a sop to a dying man…?'

She reached up and took his face between her hands. Tears stood out in her eyes as she fixed him with a fierce glare. 'I don't want to talk about that!' she breathed. 'I've never seen anyone as alive as you are—and, for the record, there is nothing at all selfless about what I'm doing.'

Rafiq searched her face, and from the expression of predatory satisfaction that slowly spread across his bronzed features she could only assume he was satisfied with what he saw reflected there.

By some miracle he managed to keep his passion on its leash, though the immense effort made him shake like a highly strung racehorse in the slips.

'You know that I can offer you no future?' He refused to allow himself to think of what might have been. 'This is…'

'Sex,' Gabby inserted, stealing his earlier line. It was easier to say it herself than hear him do so.

Even so, the surgically stark pronouncement had instantly brought an emotional lump the size of a boulder to Gabby's throat. She struggled to speak past the aching occlusion.

'You think a woman cannot want uncomplicated sex?' she asked, thinking *Not this woman*. But there was no need to tell him that.

Her response should have eased his mind, but he looked less than pleased. Maybe he saw through her lie?

'All my relationships have been with women who wanted uncomplicated sex.' And that was the way he had wanted it. But now he wanted more, and he had no right to ask for it. He had no future. If she wanted the here and now he would give it to her—he didn't have the strength not to!

His admission had sent a jealous jab through Gabby.

'Then I'm no different.' Except for the style, elegance, sexual experience… The list of the things she didn't possess which they no doubt had was depressingly long.

Rafiq found himself responding without even thinking. 'You *are* different.' And so was he—very different from the man who had once wanted low-maintenance mistresses.

'I knew you'd realise eventually that I'm not royal material.'

He blinked, astonished at her interpretation of his words.

'But does that matter when there are just the two of us?'

He made no response, and she thought, *Hell, do I have to beg?* The knowledge that she would if need be was deeply shocking.

'You don't wear a crown in bed, do you?'

'I wear nothing in bed.'

The colour flew to her cheeks.

'And as for the future—nobody can predict what the future holds, Rafiq.'

'I have a better idea than most.' His mobile lips curled upwards in a smile that as far as she could see held no trace of self-pity. But while Gabby could admire his ability to find humour in this the blackest of situations she could not smile with him

'I'm not interested in the future,' she claimed, trying not to think about life without Rafiq stretching dismally into the distance. 'I'm thinking about the present. You can give me the present, Rafiq.'

His eyes appeared illuminated from within as he began to speak in his own tongue. Gabby didn't have the faintest clue what he was saying, but the husky erotic flow and the glow in his eyes mesmerised her into a state of breathless compliance.

When he kissed her, bending her body back in an arc with the force of his onslaught, she melted. And when he lifted her into his arms she moulded herself fluidly to him, revelling in the strength of his muscular, masculine hardness, crooning things that under normal circumstances she would have blushed even to think in his ear.

Rafiq was breathing hard as he laid her on the low divan. His rapid, laboured inhalations registered at some level in her hormone-mushed brain. She struggled to raise herself on her elbow to ask anxiously, 'Are you all right? Should you be doing this?' The total selfishness of her actions suddenly struck her like an unwelcome splash of ice water. 'Your doctors—will they allow—?'

'I do not seek anyone's permission for my actions,' he declared, with the hauteur that she had come to associate so closely with him. His manner softened as he conceded with a negligent shrug, 'I might die...' His eyes slid over her slim body before returning to her lips, still wet and cherry-red from his kisses. 'But what a way to go!'

He responded to her gasp of horrified outrage with a white grin that was unapologetically devilish.

'How can you joke—?'

He slid his hand under the hem of her shirt and skimmed his fingertips along the soft curve of her stomach and her protest terminated in a husky moan.

It felt like a long time since he had been this close to a woman. 'Your skin is like silk,' he said thickly. 'You're so soft and warm and…' *I'm as selfish as hell.* He started to shake his head as a wave of self-disgust washed over him. He was worse than Hakim. 'I can't do this.'

Every muscle in Gabby body's clenched in silent agony at the suggestion of rejection. 'Why not? What's wrong with me?'

His eyes snapped open. 'Nothing,' he declared, his fierce eyes sliding greedily over her supine form. 'You're perfect.'

'So,' she retorted thickly, 'are you. Rafiq, I don't know if this is a good idea or not, and I don't care, but I'm perfectly willing to argue about it later. Not now—please, not now…'

The room was blotted out as he bent his head.

'Thank God,' Gabby breathed, as she lay shaking with feverish anticipation. Through the mesh of her lashes she saw a golden corona of sunlight around his dark head, and then he kissed her, and it wasn't just the room that was blotted out but everything that wasn't Rafiq.

Her entire world was filled with the sight, sound and smell of him, and desire, a deep primal need, roared in her veins like all-consuming fire.

Gabby, drowning in heavy, hot sensual languor, was not even conscious that he had unfastened her shirt until she felt the stir of air on her scalding hot skin as he peeled it aside.

One knee on the low divan and one foot braced on the floor, he arched over her, while his hands moved over the curves of her hips, drawing her up, moulding her body to his, letting her feel how much he wanted her as he kissed her as if he would drain the life from her.

She shivered as his lips slid wetly down her throat, his tongue tracing the line between her quivering breasts. He flicked the front fastening clasp of her bra and the fabric parted.

To cover the fact she was suddenly desperately self-conscious, scared stiff he'd find her wanting, she adopted a painfully awkward joky manner and laughed.

'You seem to know your way around women's underwear.' And around women too, she thought struggling against the compulsion to cover herself.

Rafiq seemed to see through her bravado—possibly because her jaw was clamped so tight it felt in danger of fracturing and her eyes were squeezed shut.

He curved his long fingers around her jaw and tilted her face up to him. 'Open your eyes.'

She did, and he smiled down at her, the tenderness in his dark face tinged by a fierce predatory hunger that made the liquid fire pooling low in her belly concentrate in a throbbing ache between her legs.

She wanted him so much that nothing in the world mattered.

She shifted restlessly, and caught her breath when, still holding her eyes, he cupped one small high breast in his hand, his thumb following the firm, gentle outer curve towards the rosily engorged nipple.

A cry was drawn from her throat as he ran his thumb back and forth across the ruched peak.

'You should be proud of your body. It is beautiful—all of it,' he growled thickly, and he lowered his head and took first one trembling nipple and then the other into his mouth. His tongue lashed the sensitised peaks, drawing a series of hoarse gasps from Gabby.

When he lifted his head there were dark lines of colour scoring the slashing angles of his high cheekbones.

'You should take pleasure in your body and from it—I do. See how much pleasure…'

Before Gabby realised his intention he took her hand in his and fed it onto his body, then curved his hand across hers, holding it there.

Her mouth opened in a startled O as she felt the hard, pulsing swell of his confined arousal through his clothes.

He laughed at her expression and released her hand, bending his head to kiss her. 'Do you believe now that I like what I see?'

Gabby, her heart hammering, nodded mutely, the memory of the surge of his body against her hand still making her weak with lust and sheer longing.

Rafiq carried on kissing her while unfastening her skirt and sliding it down her hips. Her pants followed. He disentangled her fingers from his hair and raised himself up on one hand to look down at her.

'You are so beautiful, Gabriella…' He pressed a hand hard to his chest and swallowed. 'So beautiful that it *hurts*.' He looked as astonished to hear himself make the confession as Gabby was.

'You are very good at multi-tasking,' she breathed against his lips.

He lifted his head, breathing hard, and flashed a white grin. 'I am good at many things.' Her blush drew a delighted throaty laugh from him. 'But sadly very out of practice.'

Because of his illness? She pushed aside the thought, and wondered what constituted 'out of practice' to Rafiq. A week? A month?

'Don't worry,' she said, literally shaking with need. 'I'm not a tough audience.'

Rafiq's eyes darkened as he read the glow of need in her cerulean eyes. He stood up, drawing a protest from Gabby, who drew herself up on her knees to cling to his leg. She let go and settled back with a sigh as he began tearing off his clothes with flattering urgency.

After fighting his way out of his shirt he flung it over his shoulder, minus any buttons. His body had the sort of perfection that she had always imagined did not exist outside the creative powers of an artist. But he was no cold statue. And no artist, no matter how skilful, could have reproduced the earthy sexuality he projected.

His skin was an even gold, and as he stood in a pool of warm light it gleamed like oiled silk. The muscles in his upper body were impressively developed, and there was no surplus fat to mar the perfect muscular definition of his washboard-flat belly.

Holding her eyes, he unbuckled the belt of his trousers and let them fall. A moment later he kicked aside his shorts and sat on the side of the bed.

The breath snagged in her aching throat as her eyes slid down his body. She swallowed and looked away quickly when she reached his pulsating manhood.

He laughed and said, 'You are allowed to look

and touch.' The smile died from his lips and he added in a hard, driven tone, 'Touch me, Gabriella. I need to feel your hands on me. I have been needing it from the moment I laid eyes on you.'

The raw need in his voice sent a fierce thrill through Gabby. She reached out and laid her hand on the hair-roughened skin of his chest. Then, leaning up, she kissed him on the mouth—a deep kiss with all of her heart in it. A soft fractured moan drifted from deep within her as they touched for the first time skin to skin, her breasts crushed against his chest. She ran her hands over his muscled thigh, then softly her fingers curled over his engorged shaft. The breath left her lungs in a shaky gasp of wonder.

The thought of all of him inside her burnt away the last threads of Gabby's control. She felt liberated. She felt alive.

His mouth was against hers. He was speaking— they were both speaking, but not necessarily in the same language. Their jerky, disconnected words were interspersed with frantic touching, hungry kisses and hoarse moans.

Gabby clung tight when Rafiq wrapped his arms around her and fell backwards, pulling her down on top of him as the silk cushions fell on the floor.

The tortured need throbbing inside him threatened his control as she pressed her lovely firm breasts against his chest and whispered, 'Please make it stop hurting, Rafiq.'

He held her hips and flipped her over, pulling her underneath him, and then he raised himself on one elbow and looked down into her face. Her pink lips were swollen, and in her big eyes the blue was only a thin band around her dilated pupils.

Gabby's heart was pounding so hard she wouldn't have heard if Rafiq had chosen that moment to speak. But he didn't. Without saying a word, his eyes burning into her, he took her wrists and pinioned them either side of her head.

He released one hand to stroke her, his fingers sliding over the damp skin of her hip and thigh while his knee nudged her legs apart. His fingers moved to her inner thighs, gradually moving with torturous slowness until he touched the moist heat between her legs.

Rafiq's body shuddered with the effort of not plunging straight into her sweet, wet heat. He watched her pale body writhe as he touched her, heard the fractured little sobs in her throat as she cried his name over and over, and it raised the heat roaring in his blood to fever pitch.

No woman had ever been so sensitive to his touch. He had never wanted to please a woman more. He had never wanted to possess a woman more. He shook quite literally with raw need. His nostrils flared as he bent his head and ran his tongue down the soft curve of her belly, smelling the scent of her arousal, breathing it in deeply.

Gabby's teeth sank deep into her lower lip. She could taste blood in her mouth but barely registered it as his fingers stroked her, flicking across her tight nub, driving her to the brink before sliding into her smooth slickness.

Her cheeks flushed bright, she was delirious with pleasure.

'You're so tight,' he murmured, biting softly into the curve of her neck, kissing the corner of her mouth, and her eyelids as he finally settled between her legs, the silky hard tip of his erection nudging her.

Then he was inside her. One long, deep thrust buried him deep in her very core. Gabby's untutored body convulsed with shock at this new and most shocking of all sensations, and above her Rafiq stilled.

Gabby, her senses glutted with new sensations, barely registered the cry that was torn from his throat. Rafiq was filling her, stretching her, and when he moved, sinking in and withdrawing over and over, pushing deeper, touching the core of her, she lost all sense of self. All that was left was primal driving need and Rafiq.

When the climax hit her she called his name and clung to him. She felt close to losing consciousness as every pleasure-soaked cell of her body exploded. She heard him cry her name and felt the hot rush of his own release. They lay there, their sweat-slick bodies entwined, gasping for air.

Slowly reality seeped back, and Rafiq began to pull away.

'No!' she cried, throwing her arms across his broad back.

Rafiq turned his head to angle a questioning look into her flushed face. She looked like a wanton angel, her lips red and wet, her smooth cheeks flushed, her eyes bright and her wild blonde hair spread out on the bright silk pillows.

'Can we just stay like this for a little while?' she coaxed. 'You don't have to do anything, just…' She lowered her eyes and stroked his back. His skin felt like satin. 'You feel so good… Just a little while…please?'

Her wide eyes flew to his face as she felt him pulse inside her. 'Well, we *could* do something— if you like?'

He fixed her with a smouldering stare. 'Yes, you little witch—I like,' he growled. 'I have never felt this alive in my life.'

The second time was slower, their passion tinged with a sweet, aching tenderness that brought tears to her eyes—tears that overflowed when her climax claimed her. Rafiq accepted the tears and held her, rocking her back and forth slowly until they abated.

CHAPTER THIRTEEN

THEIR lovemaking had been meant as a brief escape, a mechanical exercise—not something that was life-affirming, a confirmation that he was alive.

Rafiq had never wanted to live so much in his life!

As their sweat-slick bodies cooled his brain started functioning again, and he was furious with himself for allowing his emotions to become involved. Once he had called himself every word for a total bastard in his multilingual vocabulary his anger shifted to Gabriella—Gabriella, who had deceived him. Even now he could not believe that it was possible. There was a dream-like quality to the entire experience— he was living a forbidden fantasy.

Looking down at her tousled blonde head, he felt his anger slide away. Something twisted in his chest: a pain he avoided analysing. He smoothed down her hair, soft like silk. He breathed in the scent of her skin. It smelt of roses and of her and of him.

His arms tightened around her warm, pliant body,

and she made a little noise in her throat like a contented kitten.

'Sorry about the crying, Rafiq.' Gabby was grateful that he hadn't asked her to explain the overflow of emotions. 'Thank you,' she whispered, kissing his hand.

His racing mind slowed as he let her softness seep into him. He didn't want to move and he didn't want to think—because this was one conversation he didn't want to have. Not yet.

He ought to feel ashamed—well, he did. But the emotion was submerged beneath layer on layer of gloating male satisfaction. She was *his*.

In his arms she stirred again, running a hand down his hair-roughened chest and then circling his pebble-hard flat male nipple with her fingertip. The lustful surge of his body made it clear that if he put off the conversation much longer it wasn't going to happen for some time.

'How is this possible, Gabriella?'

With lazy, cat-like grace Gabby, who had been lying with her back curved into his chest, rolled over onto her stomach, sending a shower of silk cushions cascading onto the floor.

She propped herself up on one elbow, and with one hand under her chin looked enquiringly into his face.

'I was just asking myself the same thing,' she admitted. She knew he wanted this to be straightforward sex, but unable to stop herself, and frankly not caring if she came across as besotted and hero worshipping, she added huskily. 'That was—you are—utterly and totally incredible.'

'And you were a virgin,' he charged grimly.

While his shock and horror at the moment of discovery had been almost instantly swamped by an elemental surge of primal gratification that he was her first lover it was now back in spades.

Gabby blinked as she registered the simmering outrage in his voice and manner. His reaction struck her as extremely unreasonable. What was she meant to do? Deny it? Or produce some sort of defence?

'That bothers you?'

'Bothers me?' he echoed incredulously. 'What do you think? A woman of your age would normally have had many lovers.'

'You're the one with the file on me. You knew I didn't have a boyfriend. You said—'

'No man in your life at present,' he cut in. 'I knew you had not had a long-term relationship or a live-in lover, not never had sex! It genuinely never even crossed my mind that a woman who looks like you, who is so obviously passionate...' He rolled onto his back and propped a hand under his head. 'And last night I saw my brother climb into your bed.'

'Bedroom—not bed. Big difference. It's not my fault if you have a smutty imagination.' *He thinks I'm beautiful!* Gabby struggled to get her head around this amazing fact.

'This is not something you were complaining about earlier.'

Gabby turned a reproachful look on him.

'What is this? An interrogation? Hakim and I just chatted.'

'Chatted?' Rafiq echoed. 'You *chatted*?' It was inexplicable to him that any man could be in her bedroom and just chat.

'I didn't say we had sex. You just assumed…'

'You wanted me to assume.'

The accusation struck Gabby as deeply unfair. 'I hardly think you are in any position to criticise me. It's not my fault you were spying on me.'

'Do not be ridiculous!'

It was the first time she could recall Rafiq dodging her gaze. A sure sign of guilt.

'I did try to tell you nothing happened. You refused to listen.' Gabby glared at him. He had spoilt everything and her mellow glow of contentment had vanished.

And sex didn't seem to have made him very happy either, she thought, studying his face and noticing for the first time the greyish tinge beneath the surface of his usually vibrant skin.

Fear rushed through her. During the time when she had been in his arms, when they had been one, she had forgotten. Now the fear came rushing back.

'Oh, my God—this is all my fault.' She scrabbled into a kneeling position and began to pull the silken throw that had slipped to the floor over him.

Rafiq caught her hand and trapped it under his as he pressed it flat on his belly.

Her fingers spread and flexed as contact with his hair-roughened skin made things stir and shift lustfully deep inside her. What sort of woman did that make her? He was ill, and all she could think about was sex.

'What are you doing?'

Gabby shook her head. 'I don't know. I make a pretty clueless nurse,' she admitted ruefully. 'Can I get you something? Water and an aspirin…?' She lifted a hand to her head and groaned remorsefully. 'I'm so selfish. You should be conserving your strength, not…'

His smile was tinged with tenderness as he watched the blush spread across her face. His teasing expression abruptly faded. 'Not stealing your virginity?'

She squeezed her eyes tight shut and groaned. 'I don't know why you're acting like this is such a big deal. It was hardly stealing—I virtually begged you.'

'I'm not ill, Gabriella. I just didn't get much sleep last night.' Not much as in practically none. Rafiq had spent the night torturing himself, thinking of her in his brother's arms.

'Are you sure?'

He nodded.

'And do you expect to get much sleep tonight?'

Encouraged by his audible sharp intake of breath, she threw him a look of provocative challenge and, holding his eyes, ran a finger down the hard plane of his chest, before spreading her fingers across the hair-roughened skin of his washboard-hard belly, then lower.

'Stop that!' he growled, and Gabby stopped smiling.

The indentation between her brows deepened as her blue gaze fluttered questioningly to his face. 'What's wrong?'

'You can ask me that?' He sounded amazed and inexplicably angry as he lifted a hand and tucked it under his head. Refusing to acknowledge the hurt bewilderment in her eyes, his own eyes slipped downwards to the gentle sway of her coral-tipped breasts. He swore, and snapped, 'For pity's sake put some clothes on.'

Gabby flinched as though he had struck her. His words had made her feel painfully self-conscious of her nakedness—a nakedness that moments earlier had felt empowering and natural.

'Why? Don't I come up to your high standards?' she asked, grabbing the cover she had draped over him and wrapping it around her own shoulders.

He looked at her as though she was insane. 'Because I can't think with your breasts in my face.' He couldn't think anyway. His brain was still refusing to move beyond the shock that she'd been a virgin.

Gabby blinked, and blushed again as her eyes slid to the tell-tale imprint of his arousal stirring beneath the fine silk covering.

'Oh!' she said, feeling slightly mollified. She was no expert, but for a man who was not in the most robust of health he appeared to have remarkable stamina. 'Is that a problem? You could think later.'

'You appear not to appreciate the seriousness of this situation.'

'*What* situation?'

'You were an innocent.'

'I realise that in your world not being a virgin lowers my market value, but in my world... Dear God, the way you're talking anyone would think I was pregnant.'

Rafiq froze. 'You could be.' He struck the heel of his hand to his head and groaned.

Watching him, Gabby was distracted by the rippling contraction of his stomach muscles as he sat upright in one fluid flowing motion. She watched covetously as he swung his legs over the side of the divan and continued to display a total lack of self-consciousness over his naked state.

'Could be?' she echoed vaguely.

'Of course you could be. You're not taking contraception.' Virgins did not need to. His voice was heavy with self-recrimination as he added, 'And I didn't take precautions.'

That this was the first time in his life he had been so criminally careless would not by his reckoning be a comfort to her, and it was certainly no excuse. There *was* no excuse!

Gabby opened her mouth to tell him he could relax, that there was no chance she was pregnant. Not that she had shown any more care of the consequences than he had. It was by pure chance not cautious foresight that she happened to be protected. She had started taking the contraceptive pill the previous month, when her doctor had prescribed it in the hope of regulating her irregular and painful periods.

Instead she heard herself say, 'Look, even if I was it wouldn't be the end of the world.'

He looked at her as though she had lost her mind. 'A life, a child, can never be dismissed so carelessly.'

She flushed at the reprimand. 'There is no child.'

'I don't think you have thought about the implications. If you are pregnant, the child would be heir to the throne.'

'Great—let's get married on the off-chance!'

He responded to her sarcasm with a nod of agreement. 'Obviously the child would only be heir if he was legitimate.'

Gabby couldn't believe what she was hearing. 'It might be a girl.'

He dismissed the possibility with a regal wave of his hand. The response drew a choked laugh from Gabby.

'Do you realise how crazy this is? We're discussing a child that doesn't even exist.'

'Maybe not now,' he continued, speaking his thoughts aloud, 'but it could. I have months to live yet.'

His unemotional observation sent a chill down Gabby's spine.

'I don't know why I haven't thought of this before,' he said.

Gabby couldn't believe he was suggesting what it sounded like. 'Possibly because you were still in touch with reality then?'

'It would secure the future of the throne. My father would guide you when the time comes—you would be regent for our son.'

She could almost see the scheme forming in his head. 'You have it all planned out, then?'

Her tone brought his attention to her face. 'Have I said something wrong?'

She arched a brow and hugged the throw tighter around her body. 'What could be wrong? I'm delighted if this little oversight might result in a solution to your heir problem. A sort of two birds with one stone scenario?' She swung her legs off the opposite side of the divan and sat with her back to him. 'My God, you're discussing a child that doesn't even exist—and thank God it doesn't. I've always thought that people who have a baby to paper over the cracks in a marriage are selfish and misguided, but this isn't just misguided—it's terribly wrong. Babies should be born out of *love*!'

'You're being emotional.'

The cold accusation drew a laugh from Gabby, who stood up still draped in the brightly coloured throw. 'Is that a crime?'

'Statistically, the majority of babies in your country are conceived by accident—does that mean they are any less loved by their parents?'

She gave a growl of utter frustration. 'I don't even know why we're discussing this.'

'You can't ignore the possibility you could be pregnant.'

'I'm not,' she said flatly. 'If you plan to go out and impregnate some willing incubator, fine! But personally I'd like the man I'm in bed with to be thinking of me, not of securing political stability for his country. Call me an old romantic, but there it is.'

As she spoke, Rafiq's face darkened. 'Have you quite finished?'

Gabby shrugged and began to walk away, but Rafiq bounded to his feet and spun her back to him.

'You have so much experience with being in bed with men?'

'I've had a shaky start,' she admitted. 'But I live in hope.' Actually, hope was in pretty short supply.

'You provoke me, Gabriella.' His hands slid down her shoulders, effectively clamping her arms to her sides as he yanked her towards him. It was defiance alone that enabled Gabby to hold his gaze as his smouldering eyes moved across her upturned features. 'If I could have thought of *anything* but you when we were making love…' He paused, sucking in a deep breath. 'If I could have thought of anything but burying myself in your body we would not be discussing the possibility of a child now.'

The earthy admission sent a thrill through her receptive body.

'As for me seeking a willing…what was your word?' He arched a sardonic brow. 'Ah, yes, incubator. That is not going to happen.' He felt some of the tension slip from her shoulders. 'I am angry with myself, not you.'

'That makes two of us,' Gabby said, feeling a little soothed but still very raw emotionally.

With an arm around her shoulder he led her back to the divan. 'Your first lover should not be someone like me who is not…who is not in it for the long haul,' he finished, with a dry laugh that broke her heart. 'And I could have left you with a child. What if something happens to me before you even know for sure?'

She shook her head in fierce rejection. 'It won't.' *It can't.*

'We have to consider the possibility.'

Gabby shook her head mutely, unsure she could speak for long enough now to explain exactly why she couldn't be pregnant without bursting into tears.

'The only way I know to protect you is for us to get married. Even with no baby, you were an innocent.'

She looked up, aghast, her brain working slowly to process the reality that he had just proposed marriage.

'You asked me to be selfish and say what I wanted. I want this.'

'Moral blackmail really is your forte, isn't it, Rafiq? Just tell me—if there was no baby, if there never *would* be a baby, would you still want to marry me?'

She was totally confident of his answer. Rafiq's survival instincts had kicked in—not for himself, but for his country. He had been taught from birth that the wellbeing of an entire land and people were his responsibility, and now all his energies were focused on that end. This was about a baby, an heir.

'Yes.'

Her face fell. *'Yes?'*

He held her eyes and said again firmly, 'Yes.'

'But *why*?'

'The only woman I wish to sleep with is you. I was hoping that this was an experience you would like to repeat.' Finger under her chin, he tilted her face up to his. 'If it helps, my motivation is not political—just sexual.'

'You know I want to sleep with you again,' she said, her eyes filling with tears. 'Damn!' she muttered, brushing them away with the back of her hand. 'I never cry. But we can sleep together without getting married.'

'You were an innocent and that changes matters. You could be carrying my child.'

'You want me to be?'

He didn't deny it.

'It would make you happy?'

He stilled and scanned her face, sensing a change in her attitude but unable to pin it down. 'Of course it would,' he agreed.

Suddenly it seemed simple.

Wasn't that what she wanted to do? Make the man she loved happy? If she wasted that opportunity she would never be able to forgive herself. All it would take was a tiny lie. He would never know and he would be happy—she could live with the guilt. She could live with him asking her to marry him out of a sense of duty because she knew that the only way Rafiq was going to do something for himself would be if he could justify it as being for the greater good!

'Fine. If you still want me to, I will marry you.'

Part of Gabby wished she could truly do what he

wanted. But how could she? A child should be the result of love. And their child would have the crushing responsibility that had been Rafiq's burden all his life. Their child would have no father to support him and guide him.

He expelled a long sigh. 'That is a sensible decision.'

She laughed, and he looked at her oddly. 'It doesn't feel like that. I have one condition.' *That you love me*, she wanted to say, but didn't.

He looked wary. 'Condition?'

'That nobody knows.'

'Knows when you become pregnant?'

Gabby felt a stab of guilt but did not lower her gaze.

'That might not happen, Rafiq,' she said quietly. It would not happen, because Gabby would not allow it to happen, but while Rafiq thought it might there was a chance of him actually snatching a little of the happiness he deserved.

The alternative was Rafiq spending the precious time he had left striving to achieve the impossible—to groom his brother to replace him. The fact was some people really *were* indispensable—and Rafiq was one of them.

'I know that, Gabriella.'

He knew it, but she could see in his face he didn't believe it. Was she doing the right thing?

'What is your condition?'

'That nobody knows that we are married.'

That way, afterwards… She pushed past the protective mental block that slid into place every time she thought of losing Rafiq. She had to think ahead. Afterwards she could simply go back home. There would be no need for anyone to know they had been married. She didn't want to gain anything from Rafiq's death; she just wanted to creep away when the time came and lick her wounds.

She refused to acknowledge the wave of crushing despair that washed over her. Time later for her to grieve. Now her priority had to be making Rafiq happy.

Rafiq was shaking his head, his expression discontented. 'But if we live as lovers here my people are going to think you are my mistress,' he protested, visibly unhappy with the prospect.

Her shoulders lifted. 'So?'

'But they would—'

'You've had mistresses before.' It wasn't a subject she much liked to think about.

'I've had lovers.'

'And they stayed here sometimes?'

'Yes,' he conceded irritably, 'in my private quarters. My father never met any of them. They never attended any official engagements.'

'Well, I'm hopeless at official engagements, so where is the difference?'

'A world of difference. You will be my *wife*.'

'Are you saying that your mistress would not be treated with respect?' Gabby knew that his people would not dare be anything else but respectful—at least to her face. But this was a society where women were still split into two distinct camps: wives and mistresses.

'Of course not. But—'

'There are no buts about it, Rafiq,' she said quietly. 'This is a deal-breaker. I want a secret quiet civil ceremony.'

He looked unhappy but resigned as he admitted 'My wedding would be a full state occasion.'

'And they can't be thrown together in five minutes.'

'True,' he conceded.

'And you need to conserve your strength.'

'For making our baby.'

Gabby agreed, guilt stabbing her, but a clear conscience was a luxury she could not afford. If lie was what it took to make the time he had left happy, she would lie. To make Rafiq happy she would have done a lot worse.

CHAPTER FOURTEEN

THE civil ceremony took place the next day in a neighbouring state. They flew straight back and were in the palace just as the sun was setting over the desert.

Gabby discovered that her things had been moved to Rafiq's private apartment during their absence. A beautifully prepared supper was laid out on the terrace.

'This is lovely,' she said, picking up one of the rose petals that had been scattered artfully across the white linen cloth.

To Rafiq her manner was not that of a wife but of a polite child, saying the right thing. As he pulled her chair back for her to take a seat he bent forward, his lips brushing her ear as he voiced the question that had been building inside him all day.

'Are you regretting it?'

At his question she turned her head, her startled eyes wide. 'No!'

The response was immediate enough to soothe

his fears slightly. It did not alter the fact that she had barely said a word all day, and nothing at all during the flight back in his private jet. When he had caught her looking pensive she had smiled, but the smile had never touched her eyes.

Rafiq was very conscious that theirs had not been the sort of wedding most girls dreamed of. Even he had found the civil ceremony painfully impersonal. It was hard to tell what Gabby had thought of it. She had made her responses like a sleep walker.

'No, I don't regret it,' she said. 'It does seem kind of surreal, though. We're really married... Which reminds me...' She pulled off the heavy antique gold ring that he had slid on her finger and produced a chain from her pocket. 'We don't want people to see this.'

Rafiq watched, his expression closed and struggling hard with his pride, as she put the ring on the chain and fastened it round her neck.

'No one will know it's there,' she said, dropping it down the softly gathered neckline of the simple sheath dress she wore.

'I will know,' he said, envying the ring its resting place against her breasts. 'And I have no problem with others knowing. I really don't understand why—'

'I'm just happier this way. We're legal—isn't that what matters?'

Rafiq looked half inclined to argue the point, but to Gabby's relief after a moment he shrugged. 'If that is the way you wish it. But whether you use the title or not, you are the Princess.' He laughed at Gabby's expression. 'Had you not realised?'

She shook her head. 'No.'

'Princess Gabriella.'

She shook her head. 'Hush—someone might hear you.'

'I have to tell you, Gabriella, that all this subterfuge is beginning to be wearing. Anyone would think you were ashamed to be my wife.'

The emotion in Gabby's throat thickened. 'I'm not. It's just all happening so quickly and—'

'It's not the way you imagined it would be when you got married?' He cut in.

'I never imagined getting married.'

She hadn't trusted herself to speak during the ceremony. The solemnity of the occasion had awed her, and brought her emotions so close to the surface that she had been scared she would say something she shouldn't—that some of the private dialogue going on in her head would slip out.

Rafiq had looked so incredible, standing next to her when they exchanged vows, and she loved him so totally that she had felt as though her heart was bleeding.

Her feelings had see-sawed dramatically all day, covering the full emotional gamut from fear and sadness to joy and love. Every time she'd looked at Rafiq she had wanted to tell him she loved him. It had been a constant struggle to contain her emotions.

'You haven't eaten anything,' he said as she pushed aside her plate.

'I'm not really hungry.'

'Neither am I—not for food.'

Gabby shivered as the air thickened with a sudden eruption of sexual tension.

He got to his feet and pulled out her chair. Her skin prickled even though he wasn't touching her. She turned and lifted her face to his. The darkness in his eyes drew her in.

'Our wedding night…' she said.

'A special night. But I will make all our nights special, Gabriella. I promise.'

Tears filled her eyes as he took her hand and led her to the bedroom. She stopped on the threshold and caught her breath. She had never been in Rafiq's bedroom before, and like most of the rooms in the palace its proportions were massive.

The furniture was for the most part antique and dark. White drapes fluttered in the breeze that blew in through the open doors. A large bed with an elaborately carved wood headboard dominated the room, but it was not the furniture, the décor, or even the hundreds of lit candles that covered every surface and cast a golden glow that brought a fresh rush of tears to Gabby's eyes. It was the scent.

A trail of ankle-deep rose petals led to the bed, which was itself liberally strewn with the same sweet-smelling petals.

'You always make me think of roses. Your skin smells of roses.' He bent and, inhaling deeply, kissed the side of her neck.

Gabby turned in his arms and linked her hands around his neck. Emotion clogged her throat. 'Thank you,' she said, her heart in her eyes.

Rafiq must have seen it there, because he stiffened and pulled back from her. 'Do not fall in love with me, Gabriella. The knowledge that we don't have long makes things more…*intense*. It's easy to mistake feelings.'

Too late!

His rejection hurt more than she would have thought possible. But then her self-preservation instincts kicked in, and from somewhere she dredged a mocking smile.

'You're irresistible, Rafiq, but I will do my best.'

The smile stayed in place while his dark gaze swept her face, and then, unable to endure his scrutiny a second longer, she slipped off her shoes, took his hand and stepped onto the rose petal path.

She threw a challenging look at her tall husband. 'This is our wedding night—are we going to spend it talking?'

Rafiq responded to the challenge, scooping her up into his arms and carrying her to the bed.

The words she wanted to say stayed locked in her heart, but at least in their lovemaking Gabby was able to find a physical release for the emotions she was forbidden to express. Rafiq taught her many ways she hadn't known existed to express them, and it wasn't until he slept, just as dawn was breaking, that she allowed the dammed-up tears to fall.

Two weeks passed, and Gabby slipped into some sort of routine. Her presence in the palace was accepted, and her relationship with Rafiq—so long as she didn't use the forbidden L word—was perfect.

Her main aim at the moment was to reconcile the two brothers. Rafiq had banned Hakim and his new wife from the palace, and Gabby felt responsible. She had said so to Hakim when they had spoken on the phone.

'Why should I blame you? Between the pair of you, you pushed me to do the best thing that's ever happened to me. I just wish Rafiq had someone like Carrie to help *him*. But I will be there when he wants me. Knowing Rafiq, it's better to let things settle before we talk.'

Gabby had seen his point. Rafiq was quick to anger but slow to forgive.

She watched covetously now, as he walked out of the bathroom, his hair still wet from the shower

'Would you like me to come with you?' she asked

He sat down on the edge of the bed and rubbed the

towel that was looped around his neck over his hair. 'Where to?'

Gabby knelt on the bed behind him, sliding her arms around his waist and pressing her body close into his. She rubbed her cheek against his hair-roughened cheek and kissed his neck. 'You know where. You have an appointment to see your doctor this morning—unless it's slipped your mind that you had him flown in by private plane yesterday?'

'It is a pointless exercise. What else can he tell me? I'm dying—I already know that.'

Gabby closed her eyes and moved away from him. She sat back on her heels and pressed her hands to her face. He peeled her hands away, but Gabby turned her head when he tried to kiss her. 'I hate it so much when you talk that way.'

'I will see the doctor and undergo his battery of tests if that is what you wish.'

Gabby gave a watery smile. 'Thank you. If it's any comfort, you don't *look* like an ill man.' Head tilted to one side, she studied his face. It was probably wishful thinking, but it seemed to her that his face was less gaunt than it had been two weeks previously, and his skin had a healthy glow.

He reached out and, cupping the back of her head in one big hand, drew her to him. 'I don't feel like an ill man when I'm with you.'

Gabby wrapped her arms around his neck. She

pressed a series of open-mouthed kisses to the strong brown column of his throat. She reached his mouth and stopped, her lips a tantalising whisper away from his.

'Do you think it's possible…?'

'Do I think what is possible?' he husked, tangling his fingers in her hair and breathing in the sweet scent of her.

She took a deep breath and asked the question that had been on her mind for days. 'Do you think maybe you could be in remission?'

Rafiq stiffened and muttered a curse, unfastening her hands from his neck. 'I thought we had agreed we will not do that?' A nerve clenched beside his jaw as he struggled to speak calmly. 'The doctor was clear. There is no chance of remission.'

'But there might be,' she persisted, unable to drop the subject. 'You said yourself this is the first time in months you've slept properly, and you're not tired the way you were.'

Rafiq looked stern as he got to his feet. 'Enough!' he thundered. 'We will speak of this no more.'

'But—'

He cut off her protest with an imperative wave of his hand.

'Don't tell me when I can and can't speak,' Gabby said. 'Why can't you even consider it?'

'There is nothing to consider.'

Gabby subsided onto the bed, her knees drawn to her chin as he stalked back towards the bathroom. Well, that went well…she thought.

Rafiq's anger burned itself out almost before he had turned on the tap and put his dark head beneath the gushing flow of cold water. He straightened up and shook his head, sending showers of icy droplets across the mirror in front of him.

Wiping the surface with his hand, he leaned forward and looked at his reflection in the smeared surface.

He smiled to himself. The power of suggestion was a marvellous thing. It would be easy to look in the mirror and see what he wanted to see.

Rafiq sighed as he felt a wave of remorse.

He hadn't meant to be so tough on her, and he knew her intentions were good, but he had to protect her from hope.

The idea of watching her face when she had those hopes dashed tore him apart. Better to be brutal now than let her nurse false hopes.

Dragging both hands through his hair to remove the excess moisture, he turned and contemplated the selfish thing he had done. If he really loved her he would have let her go.

And now he couldn't.

His face dark with self-recrimination, he bent to pick up a towel. As he did so his elbow hit a half-open drawer hard, and the contents spilled onto the marble floor.

He glanced at them, but made no move to pick them up—until a small box caught his eye, or the name on the prescription label did. Was Gabriella ill?

Concern creased his brow and quickened his heart-rate as he bent to pick it up. He read the label several times before it actually registered.

Gabby turned at the sound of the bathroom door opening. 'Have you cooled down?'

Her eyes widened. Obviously not. The glitter in his eyes as he approached the bed where she still sat cross-legged was steely. She could tell he was furious by the tension in his magnificent body and the ultra-controlled way he moved. He stopped at the foot of the bed and looked at her, his lips curled into a condemnatory sneer.

He stood there long enough for Gabby's spine to stiffen with apprehension. She was utterly bewildered. But along with the bewilderment came anger—how *dared* he look at her that way?

'Would you like to explain this?'

Gabby's glance slid from his face to the packet he had flung down on the bed. She didn't pick it up. She knew immediately what it was. Her heart sank somewhere below her knees.

'Ah.'

'Is that all you have to say?'

She shrugged, and his nostrils flared. 'It's the contraceptive pill.'

'It is used. I checked.'

'Yes, my doctor prescribed it a month ago.'

'You were never going to be pregnant.'

A week ago—even a few days ago—Gabby would have agreed with him. Now she wasn't so sure. It was a subject she had been trying not to think about. That aside, Rafiq was in essence right.

'No.'

He swallowed, seemingly nonplussed by her lack of denial. 'You let me think there was a possibility.' His deep voice splintered into husky outrage.

'That was the idea, yes,' she agreed.

'You lied by omission.'

'Again true…'

'Are you going to grace me with an explanation, or should I draw my own conclusions?'

His tone brought a belated militant spark to her eyes. 'You appear to mistake me for one of your underlings who has been conditioned to act with unthinking subservient grovelling to win your approval, Your Royal Highness. As for drawing your own conclusions—I'm sure you'll do that anyway.'

'So this is not what it looks like?' Rafiq was amazed at how badly he wanted to be convinced otherwise.

'Yes, it is. If you want to know if I lied, then, yes, I did—and I meant to lie. You have so little time,

and you were using it all up in this useless, pointless crusade. You couldn't let go. When you
thought there might be a baby you stopped, and
spent some time enjoying yourself. That's what I
hoped would happen.'

The brazen admission left him speechless.

Now the truth was out Gabby felt relief. She
hadn't appreciated until that moment what a strain
it had been.

'And while I'm confessing—' she couldn't seem
to stop '—I told Hakim that you are ill.'

The casual admission drew an audible gasp
from Rafiq.

'I think that's what sent him back to Paris. He
knew that he needed support—not from me but from
the woman he loves. He'd help if you'd let him, but
I don't suppose you will. Because you're so emotionally self-sufficient, so stupid and so *pig-
headed*!' she bellowed. 'You push anyone who cares
for you away. I think you'd crawl on your hands and
knees through the desert rather than admit you need
help—and that isn't strong, it's stupid!'

Rafiq was looking at her as though he couldn't
quite believe what she was saying.

'You have spoken to Hakim?'

'Oh, yes—it's regular conspiracy. You know, I
would have *loved* to have a baby,' she admitted
with a wistful sigh. She lifted her eyes to his face
and added, '*Your* baby, Rafiq.'

She saw him swallow. He looked like a man who had just felt the world under his feet shift. A voice in the back of Gabby's head was screaming *stop* but she was too far gone now to pull back. Her reckless what-have-I-got-to-lose? mindset was firmly in the driving seat.

'But not for the reasons *you* wanted a baby.' She shook her head sadly. 'No, that would have been utterly wrong. I wanted your baby because I love you. There you go. I've said it.' *Now you've blown it*, said the voice in her head. 'You look amazed,' she said.

Actually, he looked as if she'd just walked up to him and slapped his face.

'Why did you *think* I married you, Rafiq? For the title and the money?'

It could have been worse—he could have said yes. Instead, Rafiq turned on his heel and walked out of the room.

Gabby was so emotionally drained by her outburst of honesty that she sat there for ten minutes before she even moved.

Well, what did you expect when you screamed you loved him like some lunatic? she asked herself. Did you really think that he'd suddenly confess that he loves you back?

Not think, but hope. She had definitely hoped.

The first step to recovery was admitting you had a problem. Perhaps there were classes for recovering optimists?

'My name is Gabby and I'm an optimist.'

She fell back on the bed and began to laugh hysterically.

CHAPTER FIFTEEN

RAFIQ sat on one side of the desk, oblivious to the oddness in the doctor's attitude to him.

The doctor, on the other hand, had noticed the oddness in his patient. It made him want to delay breaking the news, even though he had the results of the second set of blood tests in his hand, and he worked up the courage to admit his mistake.

'Sorry, Your Royal Highness, to keep you waiting.' He consulted the figures in front of him and smiled.

Rafiq didn't notice the smile. The only thing he could see was Gabby's face when she had asked, *'Why did you think I married you, Rafiq?'* He couldn't get the look in her eyes out of his head.

Well, Rafiq, why *did* you think she married you?

It was an obvious question to ask—logical, and he prided himself on logic. And now he could see the question had been there in his mind all along, unacknowledged and ignored.

Ignored because he had known the answer.

And if he had admitted to himself that he knew his honour would not have allowed him to marry her, or to keep her with him.

He was a dying man with nothing to offer the woman who loved him but pain. The only honourable thing would have been to send her away—and Rafiq had been subconsciously looking for a way *not* to do that to do from the moment they'd met.

He could see that now.

He could see a lot of things.

He hadn't wanted an heir—he had wanted Gabriella.

He buried his head in his hands.

The doctor leaned across the table. 'I know it must be a shock, and I am sorry for all the anxiety.'

Rafiq lifted his head. 'Shock…?'

'These days we rely so heavily on computers, and the figures on your original blood samples led us to believe…' His eyes slid guiltily away from those of the tall Prince. Were the Zantaran royal family litigious? 'Once we discovered the problem with the machine's calibration we rechecked all the results. Your own case, Your Highness, was in fact the only one where the result was affected. You had a mild form of the disease, and in some cases this milder form can progress to the more severe type that we thought you had. In others it can—for want of a better word—vanish, or go into total spontaneous remission…a miracle,' he added with a laugh of false jollity. 'But that is an emotive term, and one I would not normally use.'

Rafiq picked up on the word. 'Miracle? What miracle are we speaking of, Doctor?'

'It must be hard for you to take in.'

Especially when he wasn't listening. 'Do you mind repeating yourself? I'm not sure I have this straight…'

'Of course—and I understand your caution. The faulty calibration on the computer analysing your blood samples has led to a false diagnosis. You had a mild form of the disease and it has now cured itself. I double-checked the results and there is no doubt your blood is totally normal. There are no abnormalities. As I say, I am very, *very* sorry.'

Rafiq swallowed. 'So you are saying…?'

'There is no trace of illness in your blood—no trace of illness anywhere,' he revealed happily.

'I'm not going to die?'

'Not in the immediate future. Although as we like to err on the side of caution with your permission we will organise some regular checks.'

'For weeks I have thought I was dying!'

The doctor winced and nodded, his medical aplomb replaced by trepidation as he met the furious and incredulous glare of the very angry Prince.

Rafiq's chest swelled. 'If you are the best… show me the worst! I could have told my father…

it might have killed him. My life has been… This mistake has—' He stopped dead. The computer's mistake had given him Gabby.

His desire to strangle the man was replaced by an urge to hug him.

'I'm not dying.' Rafiq, his chest rising and falling like a man who had been running, stared at the doctor. Slowly a smile radiated across his face. 'Thank you,' he said, enfolding the shocked older man's hand in a crushing grip. 'Next time I will ask for a second opinion.'

The older man flushed and nodded. 'I am very happy for you,' he said, weak with relief.

Happy did not begin to describe the feelings roaring inside Rafiq. He felt released. He had his freedom and his future. He had—he hoped—his love.

'Excuse me, Doctor, but I have somewhere I need to be.' *And someone I need to be with for the rest of my life.*

Oblivious to the stares that followed him, the Crown Prince of Zantara ran full-pelt across the courtyard and down the corridors until he reached his private apartments. He paused outside, gathering his thoughts.

He found Gabriella in the courtyard. She was watching the water in the fountain fall, her expression pensive.

'Gabriella?'

She turned at the sound of her name. 'I know what you're going to say.'

'You do?'

She nodded. 'Well, I'm not going away—because whether you'll admit it or not you need me. I'm your wife. You can't make me go away—I have legal rights.'

'I don't want you to go away.'

She regarded him warily. There was something different about him, but she couldn't quite put her finger on it.

'You don't? Well, that's good. Because I *did* take the pill, but it looks like maybe there *might* be a baby… I feel different, and I did forget to take the pill on the—'

'A baby?' he cut in. 'That's nice.'

'Nice!' she choked, staring at him. He was smiling—and not in a nasty snarly way. 'Is that all you can say? You married me to have a baby.'

'No, I married you because I wanted to keep you with me. The baby was an excuse—because a dying man isn't allowed to be in love, and he isn't allowed to let anyone love him.'

'Love…' Gabby swallowed, hardly daring to believe what she was hearing. She pressed a hand to her throat, where her heart was trying to climb its way out of her chest. 'You said—'

Rafiq was by her side in two strides. His arms closed like steel bands around her as he lifted her off the ground. 'I love you—and I'm allowed to say it because I'm not a dying man. I'm going to live— *we* are going to live, happily ever after.' He rained kisses over her face until she was gasping for breath.

'Stop… Stop…' It made a change for her to be begging him to *stop* kissing her.

He placed her down on her feet and cupped the back of her head in one hand, stroking her hair with the other. 'I love your hair…'

'What has happened? Tell me *slowly*.' He was generating enough energy to light up a small country—the air crackled with it. 'I can't keep up—my head is spinning.'

'You were right, my love, when you observed that I did not look ill. Apparently there is no trace of disease in my body—there was a mistake.'

'You're not ill?' A smile spread like the sun across her face, the only shadow appearing when she added anxiously, 'Permanently?'

'Who knows? I for one have learnt that a man should live in the present, and not delay the things that are important to him.' A wicked smile spread across his face. 'And right now it is important to me to kiss you.'

He did so, with a ruthless efficiency that robbed Gabby of the ability to speak for some time. She just stood in the shelter of his arms, feeling protected and cherished while she tried to take it all in.

Rafiq loved her and they had a future. She cried. Who would not cry when their dreams had come true?

'I'm so happy,' she said between sobs.

Rafiq blotted a tear with his thumb, and smiled at her with such tenderness that her heart skipped a beat.

'It's a miracle.'

'You always believed in miracles. It was I who was the sceptic. I should have believed, because I have seen a miracle first-hand—you, my lovely and most dear Gabriella, are my living, breathing miracle.'

The wedding party was scheduled for three weeks after the day Rafiq had been told he had a life.

It was a lavish affair, with family from both sides and all their friends.

Rafiq had needed all his diplomatic skills to soothe his father when he had revealed the full story—or most of it—to the King, but in the end the monarch of Zantara had been so shaken to learn he might have lost Rafiq that he was inclined to look benevolently on any slight irregularities in both his sons' marriages.

Hakim was there, and it had been a weight off Gabby's mind to see the two brothers reunited. Hakim's new wife was older than him, and nothing like the women he had dated previously. Gabby took to her immediately, and her small son was de-lightful—a future playmate for their child.

Rafiq and Gabby had decided to keep this news private for the time being, but soon she would have no choice but to reveal her condition.

The wedding party went on long into the night, and it was still in full swing when Rafiq took her hand and led her out of a side door.

'We can't leave—it's our party,' Gabby protested half-heartedly.

'I have a more private party in mind.'

The glow in Rafiq's eyes as he looked at her sent Gabby's pulses racing. 'That sounds like an inter-esting idea,' she admitted huskily.

Outside the bedroom door, Rafiq paused. 'Close your eyes.'

Gabby shook her head. 'Why?'

'Humour me?' he suggested.

Giggling nervously, she did, and he led her by the hand into their bedroom.

'You can open them now.'

He had recreated the rose petal trail of their wedding night.

Gabby turned and looked up at her tall, handsome husband, her luminous eyes shining with love.

'It should have been perfect and it wasn't. I told you not to love me, do you remember?'

Gabby nodded. She would never forget.

'Now I am saying—no, I am begging you to

love me, Gabriella. Because I love you with all my heart and soul.'

It was a request that Gabby was only too happy to satisfy. The only complication was getting the words past the emotional lump in her throat.

'I love you, Rafiq,' she said huskily.

Rafiq gave a satisfied sigh. 'When I think what might have been and what is, I know I am a blessed man. I have you, and I have our child.' He pressed a big hand to her still flat stomach. 'This is how it is meant to be.'

'Though possibly not rose petals every night.'

'On our anniversary?'

'Which one?' she laughed. So far they had celebrated weekly—the day they'd met, the day he'd found out he was going to live, and their wedding day—the first one.

'All of them, my princess. Now come on,' he said, catching her hand. 'I want to wrap you in rose petals and wrap myself in your hair.'

The mental image worked for Gabby—as did the wicked gleam in his eyes as he sat her on the bed. He began to slowly roll down the lacy-topped stockings she wore under the floaty sea-blue dress he had said made her look like a bird of paradise.

'You're doing some serious damage to my nervous system,' she confessed, gasping as he ran his finger along the arch of her foot.

'It is intentional,' he revealed with a wicked

grin. With a light push she was tipped over into the rose petals.

Gabby gave a sigh of utter contentment. She knew that this was one of life's great moments. She also knew that life was not all rose petals. She knew that there would be other moments that were not so great, but while she had Rafiq at her side she felt totally confident about facing life's up and downs.

A gurgle of laughter left her throat as Rafiq threw himself down beside her, sending up clouds of rose petals.

'You do realise that only a man who is very secure with his masculinity would risk walking around smelling like a rose bush?'

'Oh, my love,' he purred, sliding over her and ripping off his shirt at the same time. 'I am very secure… Come—let me show you how secure.'

Gabby did—and quickly concluded rather breathlessly that he had every right to be secure. Crown Prince Rafiq Al Kamil was all male!

* * * * *

The debt, the payment, the price!

A ruthless ruler and his virgin queen. Trembling with the fragility of new spring buds, Ionanthe will go to her husband. She was given as penance, but he'll take her for pleasure!

Harlequin Presents® is delighted to unveil an exclusive extract from Penny Jordan's new book A BRIDE FOR HIS MAJESTY'S PLEASURE

PEOPLE WERE PRESSING in on her—the crowd was carrying her along with it, almost causing her to lose her balance. Fear stabbed through Ionanthe as she realized how vulnerable she was.

An elderly man grabbed her arm, warning her, 'You had better do better by our prince than that sister of yours. She shamed us all when she shamed him.'

Spittle flecked his lips, and his eyes were wild with anger as he shook her arm painfully. The people surrounding her who had been smiling before were now starting to frown, their mood changing. She looked around for the guards, but couldn't see any of them. She was alone in a crowd that was quickly becoming hostile to her. She hadn't thought it was in her nature to panic, but she was beginning to do so now.

Then Ionanthe felt another hand on her arm, in a touch that extraordinarily her body somehow recognized. And a familiar voice was saying firmly, 'Princess Ionanthe has already paid the debt owed by her family to the people of Fortenegro. Her presence here today as my bride and your princess is proof of that.'

He was at her side now, his presence calming the crowd and forcing the old man to release her as the crowd began to murmur their agreement to his words.

Calmly but determinedly Max was guiding her back through the crowd. A male voice called out to him from the crowd. 'Make sure you get us a fine future prince on her as soon as may be, Your Highness.'

The sentiment was quickly taken up by others, who threw in their own words of bawdy advice to the new bridegroom. Ionanthe fought to stop her face from burning with angry humiliated color. Torn between unwanted relief that she had been rescued and discomfort about what was being said, Ionanthe took refuge in silence as they made their way back toward the palace.

They had almost reached the main entrance when once again Max told hold of her arm. This time she fought her body's treacherous reaction, clamping down on the sensation that shot through her veins and stiffening herself against it. The comments she had been subjected to had brought home to her the reality of what she had done; they clung inside her head, rubbing as abrasively against her mind as burrs would have rubbed against her skin.

'Isn't it enough for you to have forced me into marrying you? Must you force me to obey your will physically, as well?' she challenged him bitterly.

Max felt the forceful surge of his own anger swelling through him to meet her biting contempt, shocking him with its intensity as he fought to subdue it.

Not once during the months he had been married to Eloise had she ever come anywhere near arousing him emotionally the way that Ionanthe could, despite the fact that he had known her only a matter of days. She seemed to delight in pushing him—punishing him for their current situation, no doubt, he reminded himself as his anger subsided. It was completely out of character for him to let anyone get under his skin enough to make him react emotionally when his response should be purely cerebral.

'Far from wishing to force you to do anything, I merely wanted to suggest that we use the side entrance to the palace. That way we will attract less attention.'

He had a point, Ionanthe admitted grudgingly, but she wasn't going to say so. Instead she started to walk toward the door set in one of the original castle towers, both of them slipping through the shadows the building now threw across the square, hidden from the view of the people crowding the palace steps. She welcomed the peace of its stone interior after the busyness of the square. Her dress had become uncomfortably heavy and her head had started to ache. The reality of what she had done had begun to set in, filling her with a mixture of despair and panic. But she mustn't think of herself and her immediate future, she told herself as she started to climb the stone steps that she knew from memory led to a corridor that connected the old castle to the more modern palace.

She had almost reached the last step when somehow or other she stepped on the hem of her gown, the accidental movement unbalancing her and causing her to stumble. Max, who was several steps below her, heard the small startled sound she made and raced up the stairs, catching her as she fell.

If she was trembling with the fragility of new spring buds in the wind, then it was because of her shock. If she felt weak and her heart was pounding with dangerous speed, then it was because of the weight of her gown. If she couldn't move, then it was because of the arms that imprisoned her.

She had to make him release her. It was dangerous to be in his arms. She looked up at him, her gaze traveling the distance from his chin to his mouth and then refusing to move any farther. What had been a mere tremor of shock had now become a fiercely violent shudder that came from deep within her and ached through her. She felt dizzy, light-headed, removed from everything about herself she considered 'normal' to become, instead, a woman who hungered for something unknown and forbidden.

* * * * *

Give yourself a present this Christmas—
pick up a copy of
A BRIDE FOR HIS MAJESTY'S PLEASURE
by Penny Jordan,
available December 2009
from Harlequin Presents®!

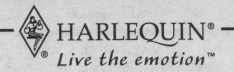

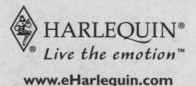

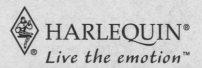

HARLEQUIN®
INTRIGUE®
BREATHTAKING ROMANTIC SUSPENSE

Shared dangers and passions lead to electrifying
romance and heart-stopping suspense!

Every month, you'll meet six new heroes
who are guaranteed to make your spine tingle
and your pulse pound. With them you'll enter
into the exciting world of Harlequin Intrigue—
where your life is on the line
and so is your heart!

THAT'S INTRIGUE—
ROMANTIC SUSPENSE
AT ITS BEST!

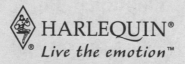

HARLEQUIN®
Live the emotion™

www.eHarlequin.com

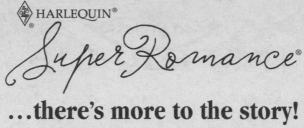
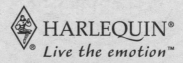

Harlequin® Historical
Historical Romantic Adventure!

Imagine a time of chivalrous
knights and unconventional ladies,
roguish rakes and impetuous
heiresses, rugged cowboys
and spirited frontierswomen—
these rich and vivid tales will
capture your imagination!

Harlequin Historical . . .
they're too good to miss!

passionate powerful provocative love stories

Silhouette Desire® delivers
strong heroes, spirited heroines
and compelling love stories.

Silhouette Desire features
your favorite authors, including

Ann Major,
Diana Palmer,
Maureen Child
and Brenda Jackson.

**Passionate, powerful and provocative
romances *guaranteed!***

For superlative authors, sensual stories
and sexy heroes, choose Silhouette Desire.

passionate powerful provocative love stories